In the Company of Writers 2007

Meadow Brook Writing Project 2007 Summer Institute Oakland University

iUniverse, Inc.
New York   Bloomington

In the Company of Writers 2007

iUniverse books may be ordered through booksellers or by contacting:

iUniverse
1663 Liberty Drive
Bloomington, IN 47403
www.iuniverse.com
1-800-Authors (1-800-288-4677)

Because of the dynamic nature of the Internet, any Web addresses or links contained in this book may have changed since publication and may no longer be valid.

ISBN: 978-1-4401-5916-9 (sc)
ISBN: 978-1-4401-5917-6 (ebk)

Printed in the United States of America

iUniverse rev. date: 10/12/2009

Graphics by Cliff Lawson, CAD Design Enterprises.
Front cover photo by Laura Amatulli.

ACKNOWLEDGEMENTS

Education is not the filling of a pail, but the lighting of a fire.
-- William Butler Yeats

The Meadow Brook Writing Project 2007 Summer Institute Writing Fellows offer our sincerest thanks to the following individuals for their constant encouragement which created an atmosphere that allowed powerful writing to flourish.

To Dr. Ron Sudol whose leadership and dedication to the art of writing keeps the program going.

To Mary Cox whose laughter, guidance, and ability to give voice to the fire, is awe-inspiring.

To John Callaghan whose stamina and talent give us all something for which to aspire.

Kathleen Reddy-Butkovich whose incredible abilities to fan not only our flames but the flames of her students, to make them burn at their hottest.

Marshall Kitchens, who brought us the technological tools we needed.

Kathleen Lawson whose writing marathons caused us to soar to new heights, and for her undying effort to help us improve our final product—this publication.

To Cliff Lawson whose efforts and talent in photography and computer graphics made our chimneys tops!

To our families and friends who gave us the support and inspiration we needed.

Finally, to our fellows who opened themselves to the creative process and acted as sounding boards, which helped us grow and become the writers we are today.

CONTENTS

CONTENTS

FOREWORDS

In order to teach writing you must be a writer. You may argue that statement's veracity, but in retrospect it's true. During the Meadow Brook Writing Project's Summer Institute, teachers come together to write, share, and discuss how to make writing an integral part of their students' lives. During the summer, MBWP creates a forum of classroom teachers K-college to discuss the difficulties in improving and share in praising the process and varying levels of achievement in students' writing. I know of no other place where teachers can reflect and rally around the cause of turning students on to the power and beauty of the written word and of the beautifully frustrating task of helping them to accept their identities as writers.

After a month of being out of the classroom and enjoying the promised rest of summer, our band of educators gathered our wits about us and set off this journey unaware of the marvelous and frightening places it would take us. We found ourselves no longer battling against curriculum and government legislation so much as we struggled to remember our roots as students while keeping our identities as teachers. It was an extremely rewarding endeavor.

We re-learned and re-framed our alphabet. We took time to think about and analyze our history and what it means to tell someone where "I am From." We even "marathoned" for the first time, and the words and ideas and possibilities flowed from us like water. We were given assignments like ABC poems and the 7-word poem that were fun projects as well as projects that we could use in the classroom with our students.

The Meadow Brook Writing Project gave us the chance to become more experienced teachers by remembering first that we were learners.

by Elontra Hall & Ronnelle G. Payne

Chimney Tops

Look high to yonder chimney tops
Watchmen holding strong
Alternating spirals
Entertaining lords and ladies
with affection and companionship
Once bringing heat
to those on a frosty Michigan night
Pleasing glowing hearths with
radiant cherry hot coals
Only a remembrance that is now caressed
on lonely holidays
You now fill the innocent passerby
With curiosity
What secrets were told by your side?
Whose love did you manage to ignite?
Why so many
so different?

Brick by brick you climb the sky
Rising upwards with stately grace
Twisting and turning
You tell a tale that longs to be told
A passageway to a point in time
That has long past us by.

by Laura Amatulli

CHAPTER 1

ABC

POEMS

ABC ABC ABC ABC ABC ABC ABC ABC ABC ABC ABC ABC ABC ABC

My Guilty Pleasure
Laura Hutten

American Broadcasting Company
Develops Episodes,
Fictional General Hospital.
Intimacy, Jealousy, Kinship.
Luke/Laura Marriage Nuptials,
Outshines Primetime.
Quartermaine Relationships Start Turmoil.
Universal Values.
Wide-eyed, eXcited, Young Zealot.

CONCERTS
April Lewis

Applause Beaming,
Cardiac Entertainment,
Fermenting Gross Heat,
Indiscriminating Junction,
Kindling Loud Moments,
Nearly Over Performance,
Quickens Roar,
Simultaneously, Taunting, Unique Visitors,
Waving Excitedly,
Youthful Zest!

Cleaning: My Favorite Procrastination

Christina Fifield

Always Bleaching,
Cleaning,
Dusting Everywhere.
Finding Gunk Hiding;
Impressive Janitor!
Kitchen, Laundry Mantra:
Neatly Organized!
Pantry Quality Rated Spectacular,
Toilets—Ultimate Victory!
What eXists Yucky?
Zilch!

STONEHENGE

Katie Meister

Aching, Becoming callus
Digging Earth
Formidable Godly Holes
Interments
Just Keep Lowering
Monoliths
Not Offering Peace
Quivering Royal Stones
Towering Upward
Vanishing Wishes
eXhilarating
Yonder Zenith

GRANNY'S CUTIE PATOOTIE
Bonnie Cates

Adorable Baby
Cuddly Dino Will
Energetic, Feisty Grandson
Happy, Intelligent Jumparoo
Keen
Loves Music
Noisily Overwhelming
Pintsized Quipster
Rejoicing, Scintillating Toddler
Uproarious, Vivacious WILL
eXcitable, Youthful Zaftig

CHAPTER 2

SEVEN-WORD POEMS

777777777777777777777777777777777777777777777777777777777777777777777777777777

BEDTIME

Laura Hutten

"Choo Choo, All Aboard."
His boisterous version of a train whistle.
"Choo Choo, All Aboard."
The sluggish wheels of the radio flyer turn.
"Choo Choo, All Aboard."
Mustard covered cheeks and citrus sticky lips can't stop him
"Choo Choo, All Aboard "
The sky turns dark.
Acrid, Change Focus
"No, No, Out, Out Train, Train, Please Please!"
"Night, Night?!"

SONORAN DESERT IN THE MORNING
Christina Fifield

The sun peers over the majestic mountains,
illuminating the landscape in a warm and hazy light.

Dense purple violets form an endless velvet bed,
as shadows of rigid black mountains creep slowly across the valley.

Tall, prickly saguaros stand guard on the mountainside,
their multiple arms waving in the air.

Bumblebees swarm methodically,
darting to and from the scrumptious wildflowers they smell.

I gaze at nature's glory,
taking in the gorgeous sight.
My eyes shift from the view and cast downward at the tire, limp and mushy.
What a fortuitous place to have a flat last night.

SEVEN-WORD POEM

Laura Amatulli

Sour Candy
A plethora of taste
bursts
over my tongue and onto my cheeks
glistening
sour and yet calming to sweet
elating
my senses to overwhelming proportions
I bend to it

7-WORD POEM

Desiree Harrison

I look down upon the azure waves splashing against my former paradise. I think of you and of what you've done.

So ironic now, with nothing being said after so much yelling. Only moments ago those vicious words teetered off your tongue and into the cold breeze, numbing my heart.

I can no longer trust.

MEMORIES
Katie Meister

With reckless abandon
He composed his thoughts
The cacophonous sounds
Wound their way within earshot
Of his swollen, battered noggin,
Bursting as if on fire
The sweet smell of cinnamon
Permeated his nostrils.
His tongue felt pickled
Had he soaked it in brine?
Memories of his decadent night
As he said "I do.

Night Shadows

April Lewis

The day had approached its end,
As it was nearing dusk,
The rancid air seemed to linger,
As the shadows bounced off the brick buildings,
Wafting down the narrow alley,
Slowly the visionary walked,
Embracing the moment-
Before what was to come reared its hideous face,
The day had arrived,
For the ostentatious being!

WILL'S SYMPHONY
Bonnie Cates

Dumbo, Mickey, Pooh and Ducky,
Always an eager audience for Will
Are all juxtaposed in front of the gate
That separates the fireplace from the rest of the living room.
Ear shattering squeals of laughter are heard
As Granny musters up her strength
To get down on her hands and knees and chase
Will around the floor.
As we're crawling around, among the toys,
The dog shaped xylophone with the cute calliope sound
Suddenly catches Will's eye
And he stops to play a little funky music.
As he plinks on the keys,
He dances and laughs as he plays "beauteous music"
For his audience
While the rest of us hear a cacophony.
Oh, the innocence of childhood,
For I know all too soon this childish cacophony

Will turn into teenage cacophony.

CHAPTER 3

Laura Hutten

I AM FROM...

I am from Paula's kitchen,
Pesach, Yontif, Sunday Brunch.
Gefilte Fish, Matzah Ball Soup, Kugel, Briscuit, Sponge Cake, Lox, Herring,
Bagels and Blintzes.

I am from,
"Can we order Sushi?" "Again!"

I am from,
Munching the leftovers off the highchair tray.

I am now from Weight Watchers, Applebee's, Mr. Pita.
Anything under 5 points, a treasure!
I am from weight gain and weight loss,
My personal roller coaster that I can't get off.

I am from fabulous shopping sprees for new clothes that cost too much and
Desperate shopping sprees for new clothes that are cheap, black and baggie.

I am from Purple Heart and Vietnam Veterans' clothing donations.
I am from marathons, kickboxing, treadmill running and personal training.

I am from a leather couch, General Hospital and snacks, snacks, snacks.
Did I really eat all that in one hour?
I am from infertility, hormone injections, pregnancy and childbirth.
I am from water aerobics, jogging strollers and rock and stroll.

I am from support, competition, praise, jealousy, compliments and flat out
being ignored.
I am from success and failure, will power and lack of control.

I am from numbers:
Points, Pounds, Miles, Reps, BMI, and Time.
I am from Paula's kitchen.
A delicious place to be.

FROM FINISH *TO START*

He grabbed my sweaty hand and held on. My legs transformed from achy and wobbly to strong and steady. His touch sparked my last ounce of energy, I felt like I was running on air. We made it! It took almost five hours, but there we were, crossing the finish line of the Detroit Free Press International Marathon with hundreds of eyes on us. It was my greatest accomplishment, until six days later.

He grabbed my sweaty hand again and held on tight. My stomach transformed from tight aches to tingly butterflies. His touch reminded me of how sure I was about us. I felt like I was gliding on air. We made it! It took six months, but there we were marching up the stairs to the chupah with hundreds of eyes on us. It was my greatest accomplishment.

26. 2 miles earlier, the national anthem played as we attempted to stretch, sardined between thousands of other runners. The starting gun went off. The sun shimmered brightly.

Six months earlier the music played outside the Bellagio Hotel in Las Vegas and the colorful fountains danced. Scott stretched on one knee and presented me with a ring that shimmered as bright as the sun.

Miles 1 through 5 were Mardi Gras-esque. Cheers surrounded us. Every step held exciting anticipation.

The weeks following our engagement were filled with invitations, celebrations, and champagne cheers. Every toast held excited anticipation.

Miles 6 through 10 flew by. We had so much to explore: Greek Town, Mexican Village, Comerica Park, Tiger Stadium, and the Detroit River. Unfortunately, the political climate that year excluded the Ambassador Bridge and the US-Canada Tunnel. Those were protected by Homeland Security.

The next month or so flew by. We had so much to plan: dates, caterer, florist, band, dresses, tuxedos, and invitations. Unfortunately, our financial climate that year excluded us from making most of the major decisions. Those were handled by our parents.

Miles 11 through 15 invited a slower pace. What was once exciting now seemed repetitive and dull. The crowd dwindled, the runners spread out, and the streets were quiet. My foot began to blister.

With the wedding plans complete, there was nothing much to do that summer. The congratulatory notes and cards dwindled and the phone was quiet. My feet began to get cold.

Miles 16 through 20 almost did me in. I hit the wall. My legs were lead weights terrorizing me. Scott encouraged me to trudge on. "See the sign up there or the tree over here or that tall building straight ahead? Just make it to there,' he'd say. He repeated these tiny goals over and over again. It was working, but I needed something more. Just then my brother, out of the blue, was on the side of the road with his girlfriend's 6 year- old son, Morgan. They were in an area blocked off to spectators. I'm not sure how they got there. It didn't much matter. Morgan shouted, 'Laura, you're winning!" That's all I needed. I was ready to persevere.

The terror surrounding September 11 overshadowed my wedding bliss. My heart felt like a lead weight. My celebratory spirit hit the wall. Out of town guests, who had previously RSVPed "yes" were now afraid to fly, especially our friends and family from Manhattan. How could we go on with so many lives lost? Scott encouraged me. "One hour or day at a time. Just make it there," he'd say. He repeated these affirmations over and over again. This coming from a man who lived over a decade in Manhattan and had just moved back to Michigan six days prior to the tragedy: "We'll win this one." That's all I needed. I was ready to persevere.

Miles 21 through 26 returned the roar of the crowd. The city was buzzing, filled with wives, husbands, parents, children, friends, and co-workers holding signs and balloons, waiting for their loved ones to finish. Sheila, Jeffrey, Morgan, Barbie, Susan, mom and dad were among that crowd. By then I had forgotten about my aches, pains and blisters. We were going to make it!

The week before the wedding was busy, filled with final fittings, hair and make-up appointments, meetings with the rabbi, trips to the airport, rehearsal dinners, and marathons to recover from. Sheila, Jeffrey, Morgan, Barbie, Susan, mom and dad were there along the way. By then I had forgotten about my cold feet and terrorist fear. We were going to make it!

Two tenths of a mile might seem like a short distance, but not to someone that has just run 26 miles. It was tough to breathe, running and crying at the same time. I was surprised by all the emotions pouring out of me. The finish line was in sight and I knew, at that moment, as long as Scott was by my side this was more than a marathon finish. It was the unofficial start of our marriage.

Two minutes might seem like a short time, but not to someone standing alone behind the synagogue double doors, weighted down by a veil and train. It was tough to breathe, bustled into my ivory gown trying to keep my mascara from running. I wasn't surprised by all the emotions pouring out of me. When the doors extended and the chupah was in sight, I knew at that moment, as long as Scott was waiting for me, this was more than a wedding ceremony. It was our future.

THE BEDEKEN

Before the double doors extend,
Before the train sweeps the runner,
Before public witness to their union,
Private vows are declared.
The Bedeken.

Surrounded by their dearest,
Bilingual love pronounced.
Marriage License and Ketubah juxtapose.
The rabbi's intimate blessing.
Only an heirloom scarf separates their hands,
For now.

The double doors do extend,
The train does sweep the runner,
The union is witnessed,
Public vows are declared.

But the Bedeken is theirs.

*Bedeken_
*Bedeken is the custom where the groom veils his bride. This custom is based on
the Biblical story in which Jacob, intending to marry Rachel, accidentally marries
her older sister Leah, who wore a veil. By veiling his own bride, the groom insures
that he is not making a mistake. A more poetic interpretation of Bedeken is that
by covering the bride's face, the groom shows he values his bride for more than only
her external beauty. Once the Bedeken has taken place, the wedding processional
can begin.*

*Ketubah
In Jewish weddings, this is the wedding contract between the bride and
groom. It is usually highly decorated and often framed and put on a wall in
the couple's home.

THE HONEYMOON IS OVER

A rental car was the target, dark-colored, long. Was it the offense or the out-of-state plate that attracted the flashing lights and the shrill siren? Maybe their four-door conservative sedan with the Michigan plate would have just blended into traffic. If only they had returned the rental car sooner, the night may have ended as blissfully as it began. They'll never know.

He didn't even hear her as she explained, "Stay calm. If you get a ticket, my dad will get you out of it. " He was too angry, or was he too scared to listen?

"I have never been pulled over. I have a perfect driving record. I did nothing wrong. They are not going to give me a ticket," he mumbled over and over again as he pulled into an abandoned gas station parking lot.

The tension in the car grew thick, only to be broken by their ADHD Jack Russell Terrier, Frankie, who decided jumping in the front seat at that moment would be great fun. They waited, but no one approached the car. Additional lights and sirens entered the lot. The car was surrounded. A bit extreme, she thought, for what, they didn't even know. Flashlights peered through the tinted windows. She picked up Frankie's wiggly paw and waved it at the police officer. Maybe humor would lighten the moment. Not the case. Finally the police officer tapped on the driver's side window. Again, she quickly and quietly reminded him of what she spoke of a few moments earlier, "Don't stress. My dad will get you out of this."

His red cheeks, glassy eyes and stiff shoulders signaled to her that again he wasn't hearing. "What's the problem officer?" he flippantly inquired.

"You turned right on red as you exited the highway. Didn't you see the NO TURN ON RED' sign?"

"The light was green," was her new husband's sharp retort.

"Sir, don't argue with me."

"I am not arguing. I am just telling you the light was green."

"Are you accusing me of lying?"

21

"No, you just saw it wrong."

Frankie seemed to understand his master's harsh tone and cowered below the seat.

"Sir, may I see your driver's license and registration."

"No, I did nothing wrong!"

"Sir, I need your information, now."

"Just give it to him," she barked.

He finally did, begrudgingly. His demeanor grew uglier as he answered the police officer's questions about their use of a rental car. The officer returned to his vehicle. The next few minutes were silent, the calm before the storm. Frankie relaxed and jumped back onto her lap.

"I'll refuse the ticket if he writes one," he grumbled quietly, although he obviously intended for her to hear.

"It's no big deal. You'll get out of it," she sighed.

"It's the principle. I'm right. He's wrong. This is an injustice!" each word crescendoed.

An injustice, she giggled to herself. It was just a silly traffic stop. Why was he getting so wound up? She wondered who was this man sitting in the driver's seat. Could someone please return her mild-mannered newlywed of only six days? She knew there was no point discussing this any further. He was beyond reason, and she was busy dodging Frankie's wet tongue.

As the numbers on the clock and the silence grew, she too started to become a bit anxious. Was it illegal to ride with a dog on your lap? The question she thought to herself, but knew better than speak aloud in his current state. When the officer returned with the ticket; he refused to take it, just as he had threatened.

"Hypothetically speaking," he snipped at the police officer, "I'm right and you're wrong. What would you do if you were me?"

As he spoke, she clenched one hand on the door handle and nervously stroked Frankie's pointy ears. Oh no, here we go, she thought. It's one thing to ask her father for assistance with a traffic ticket, but was she really going to have to call him at this late hour to bail his new son-in-law out of jail? It seemed likely in that moment.

"Take the ticket," she insisted in a tone he had never heard from her before.

He finally did so with attitude. Then she became his verbal punching bag for the next few hours:

"You don't believe in me. You took his side. I'm going to fight this injustice…blah, blah, blah." Welcome to marriage, she inwardly thought as she outwardly pulled out all the stops to calm him down.

The next morning she secretly told her father what had taken place, and because he understood the male ego, the ticket was taken care of. "Justice prevailed," her groom told all who would listen.

To this day, he believes the ticket was dismissed because the police officer had admitted the light was green. In actuality, the city attorney took care of it as a professional courtesy to her father. That's something her once again mild-mannered newlywed with the perfect driving record need never know. That's marriage!

CHAPTER 4

Desiree Harrison

I AM FROM ...

the purple skies of late November,
anxiously relocated to the watched streets of the University District.

I'm from neighbors leaving for the suburbs and sometimes for heaven.

I'm from two stories of brick that were kept together with love.

From afternoons of pretend restaurant and play kitchen
while my mother prepared dinners in our
 lemony kitchen

From Sundays of watching my father dissect the weekend paper before tensing
up as the Lions waited until 4th quarter to start playing.

I'm from hearing "this is my little sister"
and wishing that I had a sidekick that bore this title as
 well.

I'm from friends and summertime.

I'm from high school friends moving to L.A. to follow their dreams.

I'm from friends being strong after their parents die.

I'm from chicken fingers and roasted corn on the cob rolled in lemon pepper.

I'm from my special recipe for jerk chicken wings and my dad's short ribs.

I'm from my mom's deviled eggs on religious holidays.

I'm from Ernest and Karen.

I'm from a history of cancer, both survivors and non.

THE BEGINNING

Was Maggie actually talking to me? Did she want me, invisible Kendall to help her with our history quiz?

"Come on, what's the answer?" Maggie pleaded through a whisper.

I guess she would want my help. Not because I'm her friend but because I'm a reliable source. History just comes naturally to me; everyone in the class knows that. And I'm done with my quiz, but I'm just sitting here staring at it because I finished so quickly. Mr. Jones only gave it out like 10 minutes ago. I didn't want anyone thinking I was a bigger information geek than they already did.

I don't think Maggie's ever talked to me. I've been in a few of her classes before and pass her every once in a while in the hallway, but in three years we've never had a conversation, until this moment. If that's what you can call it. Why would she start talking to me now, junior year in our history class?

Maybe Maggie's finally noticed me for myself and wants to be friends. I mean, Peter would know all the answers too, and I bet Maggie can steal them off of his Scantron without his ever knowing.

I couldn't ruin this moment. This could be the start of a new me in high school. I could actually get a popular friend, and have an awesome junior and senior year.

While trying to hide the excitement that was building inside me, I looked down at the rectangular paper searching for the answer to number five.

"It's C," I calmly whispered back.

Maggie smiled and winked at me and continued filling in answers with her Number 2 pencil.

A CALL IN THE NIGHT

I hate voicemail. Voicemail makes me nervous. Voicemail is not really my daughter; it's just some version of her voice trapped in time. Voicemail means that my daughter could be anywhere, doing Lord knows what with Lord knows who. So even though my ten-minute break ended ten minutes ago, I hung up and dialed again.

"Hi. It's Kendall. Leave a message after the beep!"

"Kendall, it's Mom. It's two in the morning, and you still haven't checked in with me. Double dates end at one. You're an hour late and falling asleep is not an excuse, Kendall. Call my work, Young Lady."

When I had hung up the receiver, vibrant chills went up my arm and down my spine as the phone rang immediately.

"Bill's All Night Diner, Emily speaking," I recited as I got my pen and pad ready to write an order, all while secretly praying that it was Kendall.

"Is this Emily *Metter*, mother of Kendall Metter?" The voice asked.

Reluctantly, I answered, "Yes, is my daughter okay?"

This is Officer George Bryant calling from the 29th Precinct. Your daughter's been admitted to Mary Grace Hospital…"

The man's voice disappeared from my existence as I left the phone receiver dangling off of the counter and sped out of the diner in panic.

It seemed as if I were in a nightmare where no matter how fast I ran, I couldn't get to my car fast enough. "Mary Grace, Mary Grace…where the hell is that hospital? Oh my God, my daughter is in the hospital…"

The horror was beginning to set in as I tried to reverse my car and realized that my keys weren't in the ignition. I reached to pull the keys from my purse but my hands were shaking so much from the sudden rushes of adrenaline and fear that I couldn't grip them.

"Try to calm down…Kendall is all right, but I have to get to her. She's probably scared being in that hospital all alone." The hopeful truth but potential lie I told myself cleared my mind for just long enough to be able to start the car and remember how to get to the hospital.

Not the horns honking at me as I cut people off on the freeway, nor even the red traffic lights, stopped my quest to reach my daughter. Visions of her lying lifeless on a hospital gurney or hooked up to countless machines crept in and out of my mind. I knew they would be waiting for me in my sleep, whenever I would have enough courage to be asleep again. But thank God I make her take her ID with her everywhere, or else I still might not know where she is.

When I reached the hospital entrance, I didn't bother going for the paid parking and instead went straight for circle entrance for EMS vehicles. I think I left the car running as I ran into the hospital towards the nurse's station.

"I'm looking for my daughter, Kendall Metter. She's 15… about 5'4"…," my mind went blank for a minute and then found its memories, "dark brown hair with highlights…um, Officer Bryant I think brought her."

All while speaking to the young nurse, I was surveying the waiting room and every passing patient, thinking I might be lucky enough to find Kendall on my own."

"Let's see, Ma'am," the nurse responded while flipping through some charts, "Kendall Metter. Your relationship again?"

"I'M HER MOTHER!" I roared for everyone to hear.

"Ma'am, please try to calm down. She was admitted about a half hour ago. She's in Room 209. Go down this hallway here, and take the elevator to the second floor and turn right." She pointed to the hallway to my right, which I hurried down in order to take the elevator and reach my baby.

As soon as I stepped out of the elevator and turned right, I saw that a black male officer, towering over a middle-aged male doctor, was standing outside of Room 209. The beige door was closed. I went over to them.

"Officer Bryant?" I asked the man while placing my right hand on his arm and trying to compose myself. The muscular man turned and replied, "yes" to the call of his name while still swallowing a sip from his Styrofoam coffee cup.

"You called saying Kendall was here. How is she? I want to see her." I said while peeking to the left of his shoulder into the room's narrow window.

"Mrs. Metter," the doctor replied while extending his hand, "I'm Dr. Mackey, Kendall is sleeping now, but it's okay for you to go inside."

My black leather purse swinging by my hip greeted his hand while I rushed for the door, and turned the metal knob to enter Kendall's room. The overwhelming medicinal smell normally would have shocked all of my senses, but my daughter lying in that hospital bed occupied their attention instead.

I gently touched her bruised forehead and arm, hoping that any pain she felt would transfer to me. My ears were able to notice the heart monitor hooked up to her just in case...

"What happened?" I whispered to Dr. Mackey who had followed me inside.

Without emotion he replied, "The official police report hasn't been finished, but we had to pump her stomach."

I turned toward the balding white gentleman and looked deeply into his blue eyes in disbelief. "Why would she need that?" I asked, while my body began to shake again like it had in the car.

"Mrs. Metter, would you like to sit down? Would you like some water or coffee?" The doctor offered.

There was nothing in the world that could comfort me right now. "It's Ms. Metter. Just tell me what happened to my daughter," I insisted.

Dr. Mackey shifted his weight and the position of Kendall's medical papers before beginning to speak. What he revealed is something no parent ever wants to hear. "It's believed that there was ecstasy in her system, and that's proper procedure for an overdose of certain kinds of drugs."

I took a step back from my daughter and fell into a cushioned seat beside her bed. I finally knew the reason for my early morning panic. I couldn't move. I couldn't talk, only think.

Drugs! My daughter took drugs! Why would she take drugs? We've talked about this before. Just say, "No." It ruins your life. It destroys relationships and your health. I have tried for so long to do the right things: taking her to the park, playing dress-up, parent-teacher conferences, listening to her problems. Does she have a problem? A drug problem? She could have died! My keys fell out of my hand and onto the pale tile floor as uncontrollable tears fell down my face. I gradually turned to look at my unconscious daughter.

"Was anyone with her when she was brought in?" I managed to utter after several minutes. "She, she was um, out on a double date with Maggie, Chris and Nick. Nick is her boyfriend." Damn me. Why did I let her go out?

Dr. Mackey avoided answering the question. "You'll have to speak to Officer Bryant. I'm sorry Mrs. Metter, but I was just paged. I have to leave you now, but I'll be back later to check on Kendall." He squeezed my arm while producing a half smile and then walked out of the room.

I nodded as if I understood what was going on, knowing that I might never have a clue. Is rehab in our future? Why would she take drugs? Or maybe…did Nick do this to her? Or Maggie? Or Chris? My mind going in circles made me so nauseous that I ran to throw up in the trashcan by the door.

"Ma'am, are you alright?" Officer Bryant asked after looking up from the paperwork he was completing.

"Was anyone admitted with my daughter?" I asked, ignoring my own health.

He rose from a wooden chair in the hallway. "No ma'am. She was just dropped off inside the Emergency Room." He replied.

"That can't be it. You have to know more. I have a right to know how my daughter ended up like this," I yelled through my tears while weakly walking back to sit down beside Kendall.

Hesitantly, the officer continued Kendall's story while walking inside the room, "Well ma'am, doctors found a note on her person saying that she took Ecstasy. So emergency doctors followed procedure from there. I'm sorry ma'am but that's all we know for right now. "

"Ecstasy," I said aloud, thus engraving the word into my mind. So it was because my daughter took Ecstasy that she didn't call to check in; it's the reason why she let bruises form on her body. It was Ecstasy that caused my heart to pound in uncontrollable fear, my hands to tremble in panic and my mind to completely numb.

When I said the word again aloud, Kendall started to awake from her fatigue induced sleep. I turned to stare out the window; with all of my panic and worry and now the uncovering of the truth, I could no longer stand to look at my daughter. It seemed as if I were never going to be able to look at her again; to trust her again.

"Mom?" Kendall's voice was scratchy.

I closed my eyes and swallowed hard to keep from doing or saying anything I would regret. And as I reopened my eyes I wondered: Can love get us past this moment?

The Awakening

BEEP   beep
BEEP   beep

The lonely sound echoes off of the bare walls,
Like the tick of a clock in an empty room

Her eyes open and adjust to the artificial light
Scratchy wool blanket

Low lumpy pillow
Stiff bed.

Plastic pinching on her fingertip;
A future sign that the sense of touch has returned

Her head throbs. Her arm aches
Her legs feel weak in this unfamiliar existence.

"How did I get here?" She wonders
Memories,

Thoughts desperately trying to be connected,
like the sun and the moon at dusk and dawn

Her mind wanders like a lost traveler in the desert

BEEP   Beep
BEEP   Beep

She turns toward the heart monitor and sees her mother

She hadn't thought of her until this moment
Tears. Lip quivers. Blank stares.

Reactions she didn't know existed in a parent
Her scattered memory returns

She wondered how much her mother knew.

X-Friends

It's only one little pill. A pure white digestible dime—kids at my school brag about taking it all the time… last weekend at Kevin Rose's house, two months ago before that rock concert in the park, even the record holding teacher's pet, Peter Craig, admitted to popping a pill here and there. Why can't I just put it in my mouth, take a swig of pop and get it all over with?

Maggie's eyes revealed her impatience at my indecisiveness as she finished another sip of pop." Kendall, there's one left for you…take the damn thing already!" Even with every bone in my body urging me to drop the pill and my newfound friends, I didn't want to disappoint Maggie. As the most popular girl in school, hanging with and doing what Maggie suggests is always a good idea if you want to come out of high school still breathing.

I glanced down at my left palm and stared at the illegal circle, rumored to cause bliss, freedom and occasional destruction. Which rumor will turn to truth for me? The only way to find out is to take it, right? To betray knowledge and reason and stay true to my friends. It seemed ironic that after all of the impossible favors I had granted for Maggie—lying to my mom, stealing a purse from the mall, skipping school to hang out with her—that not taking this tiny pill would be the one thing that could ruin our friendship and my social status for the rest of the year.

With irritation, Maggie shoved the communal pop can in my right hand and urged me to swallow. By instinct, I took hold of the can but remained embedded in thought. Maggie has been my friend since the first day of school. Even if that was only three months ago, she wouldn't have taken it if the pill were really dangerous, and she wouldn't give it to her friends if it was bad for them either. Friends. It feels really good to be able to think that I finally have them. I mean moving from city to city doesn't leave time for much more than acquaintances, so I was lucky to have anyone to hang with at all, even if 'hanging out' meant sitting in the back seat of a car that's parked outside a local club.

I peeked out the window at the twinkling stars and realized that it was probably one in the morning by now. I started to think that I was holding up the partying process and began to feel guilty.

As if outside of my own body, I watched as my left hand rose and my fingers formed to position the tiny disk in the center of my tongue. I still had time to reject everything and everyone around me, but instead, the pill finally disappeared from sight as I guzzled it down with the backwash Chris, Nick and Maggie left inside the pop can.

"That wasn't so bad, was it?" Nick asked, as he rubbed my bare right thigh. "Just trust us next time and you'll be okay."

"Well, just wait until that puppy kicks in a few minutes, and she'll be fabulous!" Chris added as he stumbled out of the front seat of his blue Jeep.

My only responses to their comments were smiles as I, myself, stumbled out of the Jeep and closed the door behind me. Or maybe I slammed it, since the metal hitting hard plastic was so intense to my ears.

As I teetered in my borrowed high heels up to the bouncer of the club, I felt really proud of myself. I looked like the mirror image of Maggie, who was walking in front of me—light brown highlights, push up bra underneath my v-neck tank top, black miniskirt and strappy sandals. Maggie, being seventeen, had said for months that she was grown; now I felt like an adult too.

But when we reached the club, I shied back into my adolescence as I realized that I had no money or fake ID to give. My popularity was over for sure if I didn't get into this club. Luckily, the oversized guard of the club held the wooden doors open for us without asking anyone to show ID once he saw that we were with Maggie. As I stepped through the entrance of the club and watched all of the beautiful men and women dancing freely, I forgot that I was in high school, shifted back into my newfound maturity and began to dance with Nick.

Not the thunderous base of the rock music, nor even Maggie and Chris making out next to us, fazed me at that moment. I don't think anything would have; my truth to the rumor of the pill was total mind-numbing bliss. As Nick held me tighter and moved into a slow grind, my entire body went numb, and I leaned back to stare into the foggy red revolving lights that covered the entire ceiling. Every touch was instant pleasure, and I started to forget what stress and pressure meant. But as I kept looking at the red lights, I started to believe that I was one of them; my mind was spinning out of control. While still in my numbed body held up by Nick, a blurry consciousness reminded me of health class, a quick embarrassing talk with Mom about peer pressure, and the fleeting thought of "How could my friends do this to me?"

While still in Nick's arms, my anesthesia wore off instantly as my heart felt like it was going to burst out of my chest. My breastbone felt as if it were ripping apart to aid in the organ's escape. With the music so deafening and everyone on the same high, I felt only moments ago, no one seemed to notice that my ecstasy had turned into misery and then into a fog.

I don't remember the rest of the night; but when I woke up in the hospital, Maggie, Chris and Nick were nowhere to be found. Maggie, Chris and Nick, who had called themselves my friends, had disappeared, leaving me with no explanation for the bruises on my head, knee and arm. My adult attire had been replaced with a hospital gown, and I couldn't stand looking at those brown highlights in the mirror whenever I hobbled to the bathroom. For the first time, my life was more important to me than my looks and popularity.

It was just one little pill. A pure, white, digestible dime. One little thing; an inanimate item coming alive inside me—crawling down my throat, through my heart and shattering my soul.

CHAPTER 5

Christina Fifield

CAPTURING BEAUTY

I hear poems in my head,
Styled, flowing free.
Ideas,
Butterflies,
And me without a net
To capture the beauty within.

Receipts,
Gum packages,
Oil change receipts,
All become homes for the words,

But putting them together
Proves dreadful and frustrating,
A rather laborious chore,
For the butterflies have flown away.

Will they flit by again someday,
And let their beauty be captured?
Or will they remain elusive and free
In the recesses of my mind?

THE SACRIFICE

She stands still feeling empty in front of the weather beaten indigo door. His body, warm and soft, shifts in the small of her back. The sling tightens ever so lightly across her collarbone with the redistribution of weight. It is the first thing she has felt in hours. She has been walking for miles, though she remembers none of the path she has traveled, except that it has led her here to this door, to this place, to this moment.

She stands silently, listening to the beating of her heart and the quickening of her breath. She did not realize that she would feel so much, so fast. Two weeks is such a short time to fall in love so deeply. Yet she knows what she needs to do, though it is at great odds with what she longs to do. The thoughts of turning and fleeing are unrelenting. But where would they go? How would they survive? What would become of them?

No. The nagging urge to run is overcome by sense. She will do what she came here to do. She knows she has nothing, less than nothing, to give to this child. Her family has so little food that she only eats a child's portion herself, and that is if there is a good growing season. Her work is hard, and she is paid only meager wages for the long hours she spends laboring in the fields. It is not an easy or enjoyable life. She tells herself that she will not let this child suffer from pangs of hunger and the exhaustion of backbreaking work if there is something she can do to prevent it.

A small cry comes from behind her, and she remembers hearing that cry in the night. She would roll over, scoop him from his bed, and cradle him tightly to her breast. She remembers what it feels like to hold him so close, calming him with the slow and steady beat of her own heart. She turns the sling ever so slightly, so that she can calm him again, this time with her hand on his back. The touch of her hand relaxes the boy, who falls silent.

Perhaps if nobody heard, she could still turn and return home with him. She thinks about what his life would be like. She would work long days in the field with him on her back in the baking hot sun, until he is old enough to work in the fields himself. He would spend his days tired and wanting for food. He would not have the luxury of learning to read or write, since such schooling is only for the privileged. He would be lucky to live through childhood, since so many of the children in the village are overcome by incurable sickness. She considers this life that she leads, and quickly refocuses her thoughts on her mission. Her eyes fill with tears as she whispers to herself, "Is this what I want for someone I love so much?"

She takes a deep breath and steps toward the door. Tears blur her vision, but the door is illuminated by rays of the late afternoon sun, guiding her toward her decision, drawing her to its light and the hope it brings.

As she slowly and surely approaches the door, it creaks open. A pale man with sparkling eyes appears. He says politely, "Can I help you?"

"No," she replies, "but you can help him."

The pounding of her heart slows, for this is the right thing to do. Something feels right all of a sudden, as if she knows what his future brings. She manages a slight smile, and enters the building with the man.

THE DECISION

Crowded into a booth between my husband, Scott, and a wall, I am absorbed by the stories that Heath, the director of the adoption home in Guatemala, is conveying to us. He is in town only for a couple of days and has graciously agreed to meet with us and another couple to answer our adoption questions. His extensive experience in dealing with Guatemalan adoptions over the past sixteen years is fascinating. He tells us how he has gone from simply matching birth mothers with adoptive parents, to building the adoption home, to lobbying the government regarding the complicated process of becoming compliant with the Hague Treaty. As I listen to him, I wish that my history teachers had been half as interesting, so I might have had actually learned something from them.

I listen intently, enamored with the ideology of the man before me, and captivated by his recounting of the country, the women, and especially the babies. I can picture the poverty in my head as Heath describes it; the dirt floors upon which the children sleep; the serious faces of hunger; and the men, women, and children toiling endlessly in the fields. I try to imagine the brutal violence of a civil war plaguing the land for nearly 30 years, the broken promises of a better future by an elected government, and the changing adoption climate. I feel a connection to the land, as if it is my responsibility to get involved and to make a difference.

I picture the land like the outskirts of Chichén Itzá, the Mayan ruins I visited as a child. I remember the sad dirty faces of the children selling Chiclets to the tourists, the mongrel dogs that scavenged the land, and the poverty juxtaposed with the majesty of one of the world's wonders. I think of the heat as I climbed up the steps of El Castillo in the unforgiving July sun, the sweat dripping down my back. I can still feel the view from the top, miles and miles of Mayan land spread out before me; one vast dense jungle. This is the backdrop, my only reference, for the stories that Heath is revealing to us.

"As far as medical history, you'll get little to none," Heath explained. "What we get goes something like this... We ask the birth mother about any family history of illness. She tells us that there isn't any illness, but that her brother has the devil in him. Upon further inquiry, she will say that her brother has episodes where he will collapse onto the ground and spasm uncontrollably, his eyes rolling back in his head. When I ask her what they do to make this stop, she'll say they put a stick in his mouth to prevent him from choking until it stops, then they'll take him into the village to visit the witch doctor. The witch doctor's magic will then prevent this from happening for another month or so."

"So what do you do with that information?" I ask.

"Write down 'Brother has seizures' in the medical file," Heath responds with a grin. "The whole medical history process is like putting together a puzzle. They give us the pieces, and we try to make sense of what they are saying."

Witch doctors? I didn't realize that there were people in the world who still believe in and use that kind of magic. My interest is peaked. I picture a shirtless brown man, his face painted with white stripes, and a black stripe down his pierced nose. He is dancing around a fire, a shrunken head on a stick, chanting an incantation to drive out the evil...It is much more intriguing than simply taking seizure medication. I am becoming more curious about this world by the minute.

But this isn't why we're here. I need to get my mind back on track and ask some intelligent questions. I glance down at my list of questions. *How much does it cost? How long does it take? What is the process? What is our first step?* Scott and I wanted to be prepared for this coveted meeting with Heath, so we wrote up what we thought was a fairly logical group of questions. As I sit here and look at them now, I realize how insignificant our questions are in the grand scheme of what is going on with the children in Guatemala.

Mr. Smith, one of the other prospective adoptive parents, asks Heath about the Department of Homeland Security, and how long it takes to get the immigration approval. My mind starts to wander. Despite Heath's forty-five minute rant about the challenges of Guatemalan adoption, I am not getting scared off. In fact, I feel myself being drawn in further.

How quickly can we get our home study done? Can we take out a second mortgage to pay for the expenses? When can we go visit the country? I am reeling. There is so much to think about, so much to plan. Then it hits me. This isn't just about me. What is Scott thinking? We came here on a whim. In fact, it is through a string of odd coincidences that we're even sitting here tonight. Now, all of a sudden, our "maybe someday" adoption plan is starting to feel extremely urgent to me.

But does Scott feel the same? I just don't know. We both agree that we are going to adopt someday, but international adoption, especially in a country with a corrupt government, is more my forte. From crazy bicycle rides through villages in Europe, to caring for handicapped animals in the Utah desert, I am the one with the undying urge to see and help as much of the world as I can. Scott is a bit more conservative and practical with his methods, though he is certainly no less caring. Will Heath's liberal soapbox scare him away? What if he says, "Yeah right, Angelina? We'll just fly around the world collecting kids from all the war-torn, poor countries we can find" I can't bear the thought…

As the meeting begins to wrap up, I am eager to leave; not because I want to leave Heath and the prospect of a Guatemalan child, but because I need to talk about this. I need to know what Scott thinks before I get any more invested in the idea.

After what seems like an endless goodbye, we walk to the car. I'm in a daze. I'm afraid to say anything because I'm so fearful that I won't like the answer that I will get. I walk around to the passenger side, open the door, and slide quietly into my seat. Scott does the same on the driver's side. We close the doors and sit silently for a moment. I'm nervous, but this is too important to wait.

"Well?" I manage to muster.

"Well, I think it is a completely crazy thing to do, but for some reason, I really like the challenge of it all. I really think we should do it," he affirmed.

"Really?" I almost shout. I am suddenly too excited to feel relief. I'm euphoric. My mind starts reeling again with all the steps of the process. We need to get started on the paper chase, file applications, and tell everyone we know. That's when it hits me: I'm going to have a baby!

MAYA'S STORY: WHAT'S A DOG GOTTA DO?

Foreword:

I had been trying to tell my mom for days that she should tell my story. But despite my continual efforts, she didn't seem to get it. I thought that if I jumped on her while she was typing and barked my desire to have my story told in her ear, she'd get the idea. But mom's a little slow sometimes. She just got mad and shut me out of the office. I thought that grabbing what she later called "the memory card for the camera" off the desk and chewing it up would catch her attention that I had a something to say, but she didn't seem to understand that either. I started to wonder, what's a dog gotta do to be heard around this place? But then this morning, something miraculous happened; she got it. I don't know how or why, but when she got out of bed this morning, she stumbled to the kitchen as usual (only tripping over one of my bones today), made her coffee, filled my food and water dishes, and then something weird happened; she filled my Kong with Snausages and headed off to the office. She's been tapping away on my story in there ever since. And I just can't seem to get this last Snausage out of the Kong...

Ring ring...nothing. Ring ring...no response. These bells hanging on the front door seem to be broken. Ring ring...oh come on! What's a dog gotta do to get let out around here? I ring the bell to go outside, and then they don't even come! Who trained these people anyway? Something must be going on with them. They've been way off their game lately. Slow to get to the door, fewer walks, even less games of catch. Something strange is going on.

Today, they're in Rufus' spare room, and all they seem to care about is assembling a strange new crate for him. I can't understand why they got him such a big crate. I mean, he's only a cat, and not a very big one at that, but they're treating him like he's a lion or something. First he gets his own spare room, now a brand new crate? It isn't like I'm jealous or anything; in fact, I am completely happy in my cozy and quaint little crate in the kitchen. Anyway, who wants all that space to have to worry about? I like having everything right within mouth's reach. I just don't understand why Rufus needs a crate anyway, although it will be nice not to be the only one locked in around here, and he really does deserve to be locked up. But, it's weird though, he is older than I am, and has been out on his own for years. Now all of a sudden, they're assembling this monstrosity in his room. And they've taken to calling him "Baby" for some reason. He is a big baby after all, meowing all the time when I chase him, but now they're going to treat him like one, too? It seems ridiculous.

I walk down the hallway to sit in the doorway of the room with all the action so that maybe someone will remember I exist, and that I might need to go out and eat bugs and chase squirrels. I wait patiently; sitting nicely and watching dad try to put two panels of long white bars together. Mom keeps yelling at him that he's doing it wrong; I'm glad I'm not the only one who gets yelled at around here. Dad finally thinks he has it right and hoists the whole thing up. I'm a little surprised. This is the most bizarre cage I've ever seen. It is all white, and has bars coming down on all four sides. And it is on stilts! I could walk right under it and lick Rufus from the bottom! Oooh, come to think of it I might like this new crate. Rufus will be locked inside, and I can lick right through the bottom. He'll have no escape! Maybe this is a gift for me after all.

As I continue sitting in the doorway like a good dog, my mind is wandering to all the things I can do to Rufus once they put him in his new crate. The bars are so far apart that I'll be able to fit my whole snout in. I can't even imagine all the possible ways to torture him! My dreams are suddenly interrupted when dad knees me out of the doorway on his way out of the room. "Move it, Maya," he says as he shoves past me. Well, I think I deserve a little more respect than that! I'm being very polite sitting here while that cat gets a room all fixed up for him. I haven't even complained that I'm not getting a new crate, or a spare room. What's a dog gotta do to get some respect around here?

Dad comes back in lugging a huge crate pad. Now that's unfair! I run after dad, jumping and sniffing the crate pad. I try to get my teeth on the plastic wrap so that I can see exactly what kind of crate pad it is. I rip a small hole in it and take a whiff, but the smell is unrecognizable. Now, I've shredded a lot of crate pads in my day, but I've never smelled one like this before. This is a thick pad, with little clouds and lambs on it. I don't even think I could get my jaws around it. What the heck? Since when does Rufus like lambs? He probably hasn't ever even seen one. It isn't like he ventures out any further than the basement, and there certainly aren't any down there, though there are some good-sized dust bunnies.

Dad plops the big pad right in the bottom of Rufus' new crate. Some of my dreams are dashed. Now I can't lick him from the bottom because the crate pad is there. Oh well, there are still the sides. After they clean up the plastic, they boot me out again, turn out the lights, and close the door without Rufus inside. I guess they don't want Rufus messing it up just yet.

About a week later, mom and dad go away for a few days. This works out really nicely for me though because grandma and grandpa come to stay. Table scraps, bones of all shapes and sizes, walks every day, and I'm barely ever in my crate. Incidentally, Rufus must be rebelling or something because he hasn't used his new crate yet. Maybe that cat's scared of heights or something. But knowing Rufus, I think that maybe he is in trouble. I bet he was caught sleeping on the dining room table again. Whatever it is, Mom and Dad haven't even let him in his room once, so he must have done something pretty bad. At least it is easier for me to catch him now since he has nowhere to hide.

When Mom and Dad finally come home from their trip, they have a weird piece of luggage with them. It's kind of like the basket that dad uses to bring the wood inside during the winter, but this one is plastic. This is the strangest luggage I've ever seen. Then I notice that something is moving inside! It isn't another dog, because I'm an olfactory genius who knows my dog scents. And it isn't another cat, unless they come in more than one scent: stinky and stinkier maybe? I'm not sure because Rufus is the only one I know, and he is of the just plain stinky variety. So, what could it be? Whatever it is, mom and dad don't want me near it. I get a knee in the chest every time I try to get a close look at the thing. I run over and jump up on the couch so that I can look from a distance, but grandma and grandpa are standing close to it, blocking my view. What's a dog gotta do to see what's in the luggage? I decide to give up for now, and watch for squirrels instead.

A few minutes later, mom takes the luggage into Rufus' spare room, so I follow closely. She seems to have her hands full, so I don't think she notices I am there. She takes the squirming bundle out of the luggage and puts it in Rufus' crate. Boy, is Rufus gonna be mad! He hasn't even been allowed to sleep in his new crate yet, and now there is some strange animal in it. I sneak closer to have a look. This time, mom didn't yell at me or knee me out of the way because she doesn't even notice I'm there. I peek my head through the bars and see the small creature lying there. It isn't moving much, so I don't have the urge to chase it, but I'm still curious. I don't recognize the smell, except that it is similar to scents that I've smelled before. I wonder what it tastes like…Mom is turned around doing something with the curtains, so I quickly move my head through the bars to get a little bit closer. I lap my tongue as fast as I can, and before Mom can stop me I taste the thing. My taste buds tell me that I've tasted this before…but what is it? I think long and hard, and then I remember! This creature is the same flavor as Mom and Dad! Mom suddenly notices I'm there and shoos me out of the room. Little does she know that I just got my first taste of this new creature.

CHAPTER 6

Laura Amatulli

I AM FROM...

I from the triple story barn
Top full of hay with particles floating in the sun
drifting through the timbers in crepuscular rays
With the cacophony of sounds creating the music
of a menagerie of creatures that fill the lower story

I am from dropping my knife and expecting company
Tossing salt over my left shoulder
Holding my breath by graveyards
And blue glass in the windowpane that will shine good luck

I am from the driver's seat of the Massey Ferguson
pulling a brush hog on a hot sweltering day
From the vines and rows of Concord grapes rolling over hills
So steep you have to handpick on cool autumn days
When you were excused from school to work in the rows
With the smell of the sweet sticky juice
that makes your senses hum the color purple

I am from the rich western Michigan sunsets
sinking quietly to the west and bringing with hours

of sweet summer starlight
Sitting on the highest hill and watching meteor showers
Till the darkest hours of the night
And sneaking into the house on tip toes
To sleep a deep restful sleep

LOVE, YOUR STAR

I am a star that burns brilliant in the deep night sky
And shines quietly in the blue of the day
You have come to walk with me at last
I've been calling you all your life
Sending you messages strong and bright
Yes, I was there when you cried for me
And I was there when you felt so alone
I've been sending you words and strength all along
You learned to look upward and hold me in your heart
That's when you heard
I am so glad that you have finally come
To listen to me and finally know
That I love you

EARTH PRAYER

Earth teach me time
as you bury the rocky past
Earth teach me patience
as your breeze blows the seeds of tomorrow's trees
Earth teach me humility
as your rivers dig deep into your mighty canyons
Earth teach me to breathe
as your winds blow the breeze
Earth teach me rest
as you take from the past and make it fertilize tomorrow
Earth teach me to forgive
like the spring after winter
Earth teach me where to find the Kingdom of God
And to look within you
where it has always been
and will always be.

CHAPTER 7

William (Bill)

Byrne

A Monumental Desecration

How I am offended by the youth

Who decided to demonstrate the marvels of OXYDOL
Water nymph, fountain dweller, I grieve at your soapy lair.
Are you purer now that IVORY SNOW
Has made you so?

I sigh for your former simplicity,
As you must.
When you were captured,
Could you imagine such a desecration?

Is it the Fate of a captured spirit,
All captured spirits,
To so wear the mantle of their indignity?

How far removed is the brine of fields you roamed,
Tossed, dolphin-sported

From the muck-swallowing wonder of LESTOIL.

If dirt can't hide from intensified TIDE,
I grieve for you.
Accumulated pollution is destined
To be your raiment.
You will billow and bellow a burden.

Will it be too much for your delicate frame?
Even now your leaping and plashing
Have grown muted.

Restore my fountain,
Some heroic maintenance engineer

Return my pristine water sprite
Remove new super ALL.

Let me breathe!

Pacific University, 1968

THE CHRONICLES OF SEMINARNIA

Ever since I attended my first professional seminar, I've been a captive audience and a critic of their worth. The inherent promise in these short and intense gatherings is that you will come out of the experience a changed person. Typical hype goes like this: "You will leave this seminar with the confidence to slay any giant, tackle any obstacle and go farther, faster. You will accomplish things you didn't know were possible." In essence, you will be privy to knowledge reserved for the chosen few, delivered in a u-shaped meeting room with the best sweet rolls and cold cuts the hotel kitchen can provide. Can I then call myself a "seminarian?"

I have been in the sit-down and stand-up end of many of these goings on. On more than a few occasions, I've been the eager sponge, and at other times, the leader that stirs the seminar drink. I've endured some that went on far too long, ones in which all you can do is surrender to a sort of captive prisoner mentality and agree to everything being offered, just to get relief from those Naugahyde covered chairs. An inside joke, certain to be brought up by someone, is "millions of naugas were sacrificed to upholster these chairs." Can you develop naugahyditis as a result of too long seminar sitting?

Seated in front of my computer, I googled "seminar franchises available" and the hit total was 957,000. Not content with that, I then googled "seminar opportunities" and probably would have to spend the rest of my life investigating the 37,000,000 "opportunities" at my disposal. That led me to wonder if the seminar business is the equivalent of the fast food industry, promising to feed our psyches with only a very modest investment of our time.

Oh, the places I traveled to in search of psyche satisfaction. The retired (tired?) ocean liner Queen Mary is a floating hotel permanently anchored in Long Beach, California, a Hilton Hotel property when I roomed there. I occupied a stateroom on the "Old Lady," caddy-cornered to a very active bridal suite. Folklore has it that ghost passengers roam the ballrooms and passageways. I so wanted to meet a few, but had to settle for a meeting room that had an upward draft and sideways list, making sitting and standing an adventure in maintaining your equilibrium. At Opry Land I was overcome with Country Western inspiration. I wrote my unpublished country classic, still in search of my composer son's musical genius. It starts:

I'm stuck right here between boredom and beer
In Anytown, U. S. of A.
I look for a face in this countrified place
For anyone going my way.

What started me on this journey of remembrance was an invitation I received via the mail. Seems that these days my postal person delivers mainly credit card applications, long-term health insurance tenders, and wealth management seminar invitations. The latter and latest of these included a "Special Guest VIP Ticket" – a little bit redundant that – to attend a day with "The Donald" without "The Donald" of course, but with his good friend, George Ross. The seminar, or as a colleague of mine was wont to mispronounce it "seminauer" (must have been the Germanic equivalent) was entitled "Getting Wealth the Trump Way." The letter was addressed to "Bill J. Byrne," a combination of both the informal and formal rendering of my name. A conscious attention grabbing hook, I think. The generous offer to waive (wave?) the $149.00 fee in exchange for my attendance was tempting. It got a little better, this generous offer, because it included a free copy of Donald Trump's book, TRUMP Style Negotiating. Purportedly, I would come away from this all day (8:00 am to 5:30 pm) bottom-testing learning event with one or several ways to "find income producing properties the Trump way." Also, I would "cash in on the new trillion dollar booming foreclosure opportunity" waiting for me. If I garnered "just one new idea," and there were bound to be a treasure trove more of good ideas, I would be on my way to riches. In a twinkling, I would be able to trade my professorial image for that of an Enron/WorldCom predator on the less fortunate.

I pondered both that prospect and the accompanying brochure, heavily promoting Trump-advice. Doesn't the word "trump" connote something of an aggressive tactic? Hah, I trump you! I'm the great trumper! Take that! Egad, I've become "The Donald," minus the hair. The opportunity to be schooled by George Ross, the good friend and confidant of "The Donald," was intriguing, but I decided to put my possible attendance on what I refer to as my "backbyrner." I need to attend a "You Can Be Anybody You Want and Here Are Your Choices" seminar first.

Memories light some dark corners of my "seminared" mind. There was the presenter who made a point with our eager assembled group by toting a pitcher full of water up an eight-foot ladder in the middle of the hotel meeting room - a sort of Jack and Jill seminar-opening gambit. Shock and awe was the intent, I suppose. Having reached the ladder's top, or at least as far as he dared to go, he then proceeded to pour the water onto the carpeted floor of the room. The point he was making escaped me then, as it does now - something about wasting personal resources, maybe. I've always wondered if the hotel personnel ever could figure out where all that water on the rug came from.

Among the materials and handouts that are a part of every seminar leader's stock-in-trade is his cache of humor. Generally it is a joke with a point or a witty rejoinder to a participant. A feature of a widely promulgated seminar is the inclusion of a joke sharing time, usually right after the oatmeal cookies. The mission statement of the founder of Esalen has it that, "The Esalen Institute exists to promote the harmonious development of the whole person. It is a learning organization dedicated to restricted exploration of the human potential, and resists religious, scientific and other dogmas except for gestalt psychotherapy, which permeates all levels of the community based staff and business model." If that piece of hyperbole weren't funny enough, some of the sessions were conducted in the nude. Courtesy of one presenter, who had done the "Esalen thing," is the story of an attendee who was asked what impressed him most about the experience. His reply, "the seats on the cane chairs!"

You should also know that seminar "schtick" is de rigueur. A common ploy is to toss a hackeysack to some unsuspecting sitter and then, after you knew enough not to duck, to be asked a question by the leader. The catcher in the "u" then either answers a question or volunteers some information and tosses it to someone else. At other times, it takes the form of some provocative statement or story, something to set the attendees on the edge of their seats, expectantly waiting for more pearls. Jackie Cooper, not the actor of the same name, but an automobile sales trainer of some renown, was full of "sayins." Automobile sales persons would flock to his "workshops" and later be so taken with him that they would have several of these quotes tattooed on their bodies, usually in obscure locations so as not to scare away a prospective client. I remember this nugget, "life is too short to drive a boring (borin) car." Words to live by or tattoo inconspicuously!

Gurus such as Jackie Cooper abound in the cottage seminar industry, and sometimes you come away with a little more understanding about life. I attended several company-sponsored seminars given by Denis Waitley, described as "one of America's most respected authors, keynote lecturers, and productivity consultants on high performance human achievement." What I came away with was not all that bad – "Expect the best, plan for the worst, and prepare to be surprised." From Larry Wilson, founder of a heavily weighted seminar company aptly named Wilson Learning, I've borrowed, "I have a great memory. Only it's short!" When I supervised a company's auto show program, I spent countless hours learning about professional automobile racing and its life lessons at the feet of Bobby Unser, three-time Indy 500 champion, as he lectured me and the crowds on behalf of the manufacturer. I understand him and why he would say, "Desire is the secret of every man's career. Not education. Not being born with hidden talents. Desire!" Easy for him to say!

Seminar talent doesn't come cheap. I remember one presenter telling me that his stated intention was "to deliver one hundred presentations a year and charge $10,000 dollars per," effectively reaching the one million dollar goal he felt was within his reach. If he ever achieved that I don't know, but he was talented. In my corporate marketing days, I was asked to inquire on the availability of the prolific writer and lecturer, Dr. Dwayne Dyer, for a company motivation program we were mounting. I phoned his personal assistant, Maya – this was when he operated out of Miami, not the lavish digs he occupies nowadays in Hawaii – and was told the price would be a five-figure number for a half-day program, plus two first-class round trip tickets for him and his traveling companion, presumably the same Maya. Instead, we went for Lou Holtz, then coaching at Notre Dame who, as far as I know, didn't have a "traveling companion." He commanded a respectable but modest four-figure fee to entertain everyone with football lore and the "if-you-get-knocked-down, pull-yourself-up-and-get-back-in-there" stuff.

Evaluations, or "evals" in seminar-speak, conclude the seminar experience. I've never taken these very seriously. If the group is happy to get "out of jail" and has had a generally positive experience, these reviews will be good for the most part. As a presenter, I always felt with Horatio that "there needs no ghost. . . come from the grave to tell" me how well or badly I've done. I pretty much knew. One presenter I've worked with had a different take on the subject. He saw evaluations as a report to his boss and a continued job-justifier. He would grease the process by concluding his seminar with words to the effect that "you (attendees) were the finest I've ever had the pleasure to lead." Then, he would pass out the evaluation sheets, expecting reciprocal high praise. When he collected the evaluations, he would cull them and only send the good ones to the home office!

And let's not forget that besides the psychobabble baggage we may leave with, there are the marketing materials. These include audiotapes, videotapes or DVD's, pre, during or post-seminar workbooks, and loose-leaf folders that allow us to review what we learned and continue to live the seminar experience. They may or may not be included in the seminar price, but if not, are certain to be hawked as we exit the gathering place.

I've indicated at the outset that I'm ambivalent about the efficacy of seminar-ism. Still, there are several I would consider attending. One would definitely be an Anger Management offering, not because I'm prone to inordinate outbursts these days. Rather, I wonder what it would be like to be locked in a room with a group that sends out smoke signals in everything they do. The presenter in this tinderbox atmosphere is in the words of poet Lawrence Ferlinghetti, "constantly risking absurdity and death above the heads of his audience." Still, it might be worthwhile to see him or her succeed or fail to observe what techniques quell the rages, or what flash points invite a group conflagration.

I need to understand more of the views of Lyndon LaRouche, and so, a LaRouche seminar is, to quote an overused cliché, "on my radar screen. " I wonder if Lyndon is as pro-radar as he is pro-nuclear power and anti-global warming. Anyway, why I have to attend one of his group's seminars is because of a brief encounter I had on my university campus. As the pro-LaRouche minions were setting up to distribute his latest literature, I remarked to one set-up person in passing that I thought he was "a crazy. " The minion differed, indicated that I was being rude, which I was, and said "I should open my mind before I opened my mouth. " So, LaRouchers, after you read this, look me up and send me an invitation. I promise to behave rationally and politely.

Ever since I've read about them, I've wanted to go to a Pritikin seminar. Healthy eating has never been a strong point for me. For me, a beer and some pizza are as close to a gourmet meal as it gets these days. If ever I win the lottery, a Pritikin center will be my first stop. If there is a tough-love approach to eating healthily. – Pritikin has that image for me. – I'm there.

What I still have to figure out is how to act on my seminar wish development program and in what sequence. Will I fulfill my seminary journey and keep striving to transform myself into a newer, better version of me? Will I become the high-priest of healthy eating, turning myself into an angry, semi-starved acolyte of LaRouchism? Will I reconsider my trumping of "The Donald," get with the wealth program, not worry about winning the lottery, and pay my own way to Pritikin? Maybe a wait and see attitude may work best for me. Ferlinghetti's poetic advice is to become "the super realist who must perforce perceive taut truth before the taking of each stance or step." Sound advice, I think, for this closet seminarian.

CHAPTER 8

Kris McLaughlin

I AM FROM...

I am from a barren country
a land of wide-open places
with subzero temperatures to steamy, hot summer days
where if you smile it behind closed doors.

I am from a mother who lives near by
but not with me
who I seldom see
and a father I have never met.

I am from the responsibility
of little sister by my side
from living with a family group
in an Siberia orphanage
eight girls and one den mom

from laying awake in bed at night
thinking about my sister
in another family group
wondering if she is ok.

and from having to say good-bye
even to my sister
when she is sick and leaving for the "rest home"

I am from living through adversity
broken promises
crushed dreams
all this and so much more

I am from showing I have strength
to make it on my own
to rebuild promises and dreams
until not only do I know where I am from
but where I am going
Olesia

THE QUEST

We had a single goal on our quest that day, to find Olesia. My heart felt like it had been pulled out and stomped on when I had to say goodbye to her last year. I had only come to work at a youth camp for a few weeks. I was not prepared for a precious Russian orphan to change my life. The journey today was spontaneous and we had no idea what obstacles we might encounter along the way.

Confidently, Sasha took the wheel as we climbed into the rusty unloved car. It had seen better days but somehow still seemed to get by. I sat next to him as co-pilot. But we both knew I would be of no use on these Siberian roads. Skilled interpreters, Marina, and Yulia, along with my best pal Hank from Atlanta, were crammed in the backseat of the tiny old car. I glanced back for a little reassurance. They each smiled at me. Unfortunately, it just added tears to the sweat that was pouring down my face.

I soon realized that I could hardly breathe. All the windows were down. I felt as if I had sprung a leak. I turned around in my seat to face Hank and noticed he has twice as much sweat on his forehead. He smirked. We realized at the same time that there was more water running off our faces right now than came from the camp showers this morning on both the boys and girls sides put together. I was to feeling a little shaky. Was it just the heat getting to me? Or was it the jumbled up emotions that had been running rampant through my body?

In the wee hours of the morning our small group had concocted this plan. Suddenly the floodgate to my emotions opened. If my small group of Russian friends were going to take this road trip why not bring my own emotional baggage too. Excitement was the first on board, followed quickly by anticipation, giddiness, delight, awe, happiness, joy, and disbelief. I found it hard to believe that we could make this journey happen. I used my hands and I forced my eyelids to remain closed as I eagerly awaited the rising of the sun. Once I calmed down a bit, fear crept in. Efficiently, it took over.

So many things could still go wrong. We had no idea where we were going. We had not even left the campground yet. The camp administration echoed with power of old Russian government. They could easily still stop us. No explanation would be needed. The emotions that started racing through my mind only hours ago, now took over my heart. Fear was in the lead by a l—o—n—g shot.

We were assured it would be a short drive to the orphanage. By Hank's careful calculations we had left camp over 165 minutes ago. Maybe short did not translate in the sentence the way I thought it did. The small village we were searching for concealed itself from my view. Sasha appeared to have lost his patience several kilometers back. It might be that he thought this trip was a bad idea from the start. Or it could be that he was just fed up with the crazy, crying, American girl sitting next to him. Both seem like viable choices at this point. Truth be told, he scared me a little. Ok, so he scared me a lot. I wish I spoke Russian. Then I could say something nice to him. Maybe that would calm him down. But the few common tourist phrases I knew just would not help in this situation. The silence was better.

My head hit the ceiling of the run-down little car, probably for the twentieth time. Although my headache was growing so was my appreciation for Michigan roads. Suddenly, Sasha curved sharply to the left. Somehow a dirt road had miraculously appeared. On the cusp of the thin windy trail were two cows. They were not fazed by the car in the least. Fear was still emanated. I felt as if it were radiating out of me. Then the excitement started to grow again as a tiny village appeared ahead.

Eventually we passed a large decrepit building on our right. We later learned the building had been falling down for over the last fifty years. We became eyewitnesses to that fact in our morning drive-by when two bricks fell from three stories above. After we passed the building Sasha pulled to the opposite side of the road to ask for directions. I caught a glimpse of what appeared to be routine family activities in a house nearby. As I gazed at these movements it dawned on me that I am not observing these rituals through a window like I might back home in the states. This vision had escaped from a gap between two planks of wood on the northern wall of the house. My mind wandered. Does this family hear the wind when they are trying to sleep? How much rain gets inside? Does each wall look like this one? Worse? How do they cope with the arctic winters?

Finally we learned that we were less than a mile away. The orphanage was just around the corner. Now the FEAR made it almost impossible to breathe. We didn't even know if Olesia were still living in this Siberian orphanage. What if she did not recognize me? What if she did not remember me? I had this amazing, beautiful child one year ago. I still remember sitting in a musty room. Everything was damp. Wet. Last year at camp it had rained the whole time. But it did not matter we had such a great time together. That afternoon

Olesia decided she would teach me to speak Russian. She had me repeat "Ya tibya le blue" about a hundred times. She would say it to me. I would say it back. We did this over and over and over again. Her smile kept growing until it seemed to wrap all the way around her face. I was just sure she had taught me some silly slang or bad joke. Yulia, my interpreter, later explained that the words translated to "I love you." It was at that moment Olesia stole my heart.

All too soon the car stopped. Big, blue, iron gates seemed to form stars in front of me. The gates appeared like a fortress, clearly stopping outsiders like me from going any further. I wondered, could this be some sort of sign? As we tried to decide what to do I looked through the gates. There was a movement that caught my eye from beneath a bush where two small girls were playing with a well-loved Barbie type doll. The doll looked as if she had been handed down several times and no longer had her clothes or left arm. She was bald and was now helping the girls dig in the dirt. They stopped and froze as they noticed that a car of strangers had arrived. Another child shuffled her feet and watched a rock that she kicked as she crossed the road. She had just dumped a bucket of rubbish into the never-ending pile by the lake. Her head was cast down as she made her way back toward the mighty fortress.

The heat of the car became too stifling to bear any longer. We got out to stretch and take a better look around. That was when I heard a voice screaming my name, "CREASE ! CREASE !" I was tackled. The bucket she was carrying rolled back into the dirt road, and I was wrapped up in the best hug of my lifetime.

My quest was complete. I looked into Olesia's deep mahogany eyes. The eyes I had been longing to see for the past year. I had found my little girl. A little girl who lives a world away.

"Ya tibya le blue," Olesia.

THE ROCKER

An old oak tree stood tall
growing for all to see
moving back in forth in the wind
it gave shade to many
shelter for animals
living a purposeful life

The tree was chopped down
Cut, then expertly crafted molded together, formed anew
Smooth lines, intricate designs, created a chair to be cherished
moving back and forth, back and forth
he would sit in the chair, each morning and night
reading, looking out at what the day had to offer
sharing a purposeful life

He was a proud man
giving all he had to offer to family and friends
traveling often for work
going back and forth, back and forth
his favorite place to sit was that chair
looking out at the lake
he once lived a purposeful life

As day fades quietly
the fiery sun sinks lower into the horizon
casting shadows as it goes
searching for a place to rest its weary head
Before the light disappears
it shines upon the rocker tall and proud
bringing life back
for a moment in time

CHAPTER 9

Elontra Hall

NOCTURNE: BLUE NOTE

Serendipity
Seductively dips her fingers
Into her wine glass
Smiling slyly
Almost sweetly

As Coltrane's nocturnes
String cinnamon pearls
And lavender notes
On the shimmering breath of the evening
Strings and desire
Quiver
with the release of the bass player's fingers.
Lift the hands
and now
the fingers once again caress
Slick ivory keys

The distinctly nocturnal aroma of
Cigarettes, red wine, and muted longing
Confirm a singular talent.

Draped in a smoky little black dress
Stitched together by syncopation and subtlety.

Sublime sequences escape
Into the world beyond, where
The sun has slept for hours
The kitchen has closed
And though the last drinks have been poured,
The final notes
Never come.

Nocturne: Eine Kline

Silas' Apartment   July 14 9:00 p.m.

The letter was unintelligible. Pages of it scattered all over the young man's body. Long strings of cluttered, claustrophobic prose filled the page, crammed onto each line with no space to breathe and no distinguishable message. On the floor the young man's body was no more than decoration. Various detectives stepped over it and brushed for fingerprints, others looked around for evidence of forced entry into the flat, and still others clustered about talking to neighbors and relatives. The house was abuzz with more energy in the young man's death than it had been in his life. The tall gentleman waited patiently for the activity to die down before moving to grab the manuscript.

Silas' Apartment   July 13 11:00 p.m.

"Give me the letter! I am not playing a game with you Silas, give it to me now. "
She could see by the set of his jaw, its muscles clamped tight and gently moving under the skin, that he was seething. She had gotten in deep. He had shared his story and trusted, they had shared secrets, exchanged lies, begun to overlap. This was the ultimate betrayal. "If you want this" Silas began, "then come and get it. "

She slid almost unconsciously into position. *Always guard your face, give your opponent as small a target as you possibly can*, the old instructions came to her as though encoded in her marrow. *Oh, God*, she thought, *Silas, why do you have to be so damned righteous at the wrong time?* Silas could see her face change and began to school his expressions as well. This is it. As he moved to put the manuscript down, she saw her opening. *Strike!*

Silas' Apartment   July 13 10:55 p.m.

The letter would ruin them.
"And now...put this here, move this here, print, aaaaand done," Silas declared.
"Good." A female voice began," Now give it here."
Had he left the door unlocked? Had he given her a key? How had she managed to surprise him like this? Who was this woman? The questions all zipped through his mind as he erased the original and stood up to face her
"Hello Sere," he started. "How was the club tonight?"
"Damn the small talk Silas, give me the document!" the woman barked.

The breeze from the window outside stirred her hair slightly and for a brief moment he could see her completely, her skin smooth and slightly reflective, the light from the moon bouncing gently off of her features. The curved bridge of her nose, the delicate line of her jaw and chin, she was beautiful, and sad. He could see her eyes welling with tears, shimmering in the deathly pale of the moon.

"So this is it then?" Silas asked. A plea. "Is this really the end of it?"

"Just give me the letter, Silas."

He stood, still as a tomb and said nothing as a single tear lingered on her eyelash and then fell, tracing, oddly enough, the same path that he had traced so many times with his finger, down her cheek. He wished that he could wipe that tear away as he had others, but she had chosen; and in doing so, they were now lost to each other.

"Give me the letter! I'm not playing a game with you, Silas. Give it to me now." Her voice, at first so gravid with emotion, now came with an eerie calm.

"If you want this," he began, "then come and get it." Silas stared at her, searching her eyes, scouring her body for … for… for what? A compromise, a sign that they would weather this too, a glimmer of the thing that they'd shared before? He found nothing and turned to set the paper down. The night was still and quiet, the trees held their breath, and Sere committed to her decision. Her first step forward was as loud as Hiroshima.

Headquarters   **July 14 9:00 p.m.**

What had been found wasn't even intelligible. Their code breakers hadn't been able to find anything. Silas had been the best coder they had, though so that was to be expected.

"Serendipity. " the tall gentleman began.

"Yes, One?" Serendipity replied. Her voice sounded flat and lifeless as the marble underneath their feet.

"Are you quite sure that there was nothing else you left that would be of interest or value to us?"

"Indeed, One. There is nothing left."

"Good." One turned to leave but before waved for Serendipity to come to him.

"He would have destroyed us all, Sere. It's better this way, " One said to her, his spindly arm around her shoulder. "And besides, I think that you and the pianist need to get together sometime and ahhh, what is the saying, 'tickle the ivories' in the near future?" "No, Silas should make it guilt free. Yes?" One giggled mirthlessly and then began to walk down the pale hallway, humming Mozart's Eine Kleine Nachtmusik, viciously off key.

Outside Headquarters   July 14 10:00 p.m.
Serendipity felt her heart flutter against the parchment paper in the pocket of her jacket.

Now, she thought, *I will finish what you started Silas Pious bastard.*

Nocturne: Opus Nocturna

I threw out my arms to keep my balance. Through the thin branches ahead of me, I could see the riverbank. My heart beat triple time, and I felt for a moment that if I could touch it, the slightest, faintest moisture on my fingertips, then I would be safe. Trees groaned, tilted, and fell with monstrous thuds masked only by the sound of the behemoth's footfalls. I ran harder; my lungs were seared, screaming for rest, for water, and then the branches were gone. A confetti of leaves and vines fell as we burst into the clearing. The force of the monster's steps shook me, throwing me off balance again. *I'm going to make it*, I told myself. As I closed my eyes to dig into long spent reserves, my heart that had been keeping beat like a timpani, abruptly stopped, and time for me, froze. . .

I heard the river call my name.

My feet quit their motion and in that split second, everything was lost. They careened into each other, warping and tangling together, and I began my tumble to the turf. I felt time spread out and as I fell, I began to think about how I found myself here in the first place. . .

PRELUDE

The air was thick and moist. The full moon shone brilliantly through the warm silken blanket of the night sky. Summer was drawing to a close and I found myself increasingly drawn to my notebooks. Not the blank ones so much but the filled ones. Notebooks that I had filled years ago and stored away. Why? I'm not exactly sure. Maybe so that my great grandchildren could get a word of wisdom from beyond the grave or feel some connection to me through my phrases and exploits. But I digress. That night I had awoken to soothe my throat with a drink of water. Truth be told my nights had been growing progressively restless. I found myself more and more drawn not just to look at and reminisce over those volumes of my own hand's scratching and scrawling but actually at the substance and feeling in the work. Oh, it was horrible at first, remembering my immaturity, observing my irrational thinking and melodrama. Many times I could do nothing more but chuckle at the foolishness of my chronicling. But then it began to change and instead of just cringing at the work, I began to see things happening in the writing. In the pages turning that faintest shade of blond from age, I found myself scavenging and rescuing bits and pieces. Writing down scraps on receipts and envelopes and then, small notepads, and loose-leaf, until finally I accepted that a notebook would be needed to complete the task. It was exhilarating. By the light of the moon always would I make my most delightful and mysterious discoveries, like:

A city by the sea, built on nothing
Floating above the rocks and waves and surf
Mystical and sad it sat, a child waiting on its playmates,
never finding anyone to fill its streets.

Naive and sentimental, yes? But there was something there. Something more than just a pretty picture or words artfully strung along. I kept doing it. Reading and writing, reading and writing, reading and writing, until finally, the last book had been scoured and I found this:

There is something swirling beneath the surface of the words that seduces me.

It stopped me cold. I put the notebook down and poured myself a stiff drink. You know; Martini, shaken not stirred and all of that. The line shook me. Why? It was the answer to a question lodged in my being for decades. As I contemplated the implications of this line and possible reactions, something else happened. Almost of its own accord, my hand found it's way around the pen and I was at the table writing again. The wind and full moon watched intently as I scribbled in the tablet full of old lines, new ones. Somewhere along the way I regained control and glanced at what was I had reflexively jotted down.

> *I stretch for something just out of my grasp,*
> *Something that precedes language.*
> *Lost in the tangle of my tongue ,*
> *My English scrambled and tempestuous,*
> *Classical and Hip-hop and post-post modern.*

Upon reading this, my eyes narrowed, and I began to leaf through the pages that I had recently transcribed. I couldn't tell what it was that I was looking for but I had a strong feeling that I would find it there. Passages bounded past me:

> *Layers in the water*
> *Not the soil underneath*
> . . .
> *Bach fugues fused with Acid Jazz*
> *Creating searing sequences in separating streams*

> *Layers of languages*
> *French, German, Choctaw*
> *Italian, Greek, Creole*

Finally my eyes rested again on this one:

> *The river was long*
> *It both reflected and cast its own light,*
> *sparkling suddenly in the moonlight.*

At this, I looked up into the sky, toward the source of the crystalline light that had guided my way these many weeks, and nearly fell from my chair. It was a seashell! A huge seashell hung in the heavens. I roughly pushed the chair aside, moving to the door to get a better look. Upon reaching the door I was given another surprise. The woods surrounding my house had overtaken it. Thick emerald vines wound their way up the chimney and clung to the decaying reddish-brown brick, a garrison of trees obscured the view from the door of the windowed deck, and wickedly thorned weeds defiantly pushed their way through the gaps in the boards. I called for my fiancée in the stillness that enveloped me and was answered, quite famously, by the call of crickets violining in the distance.

I bolted up to the bedroom hoping to find her sleeping or similarly shocked by the condition of our home. It was not to be. After catching my breath from running up the stairs, I stood up and had the wind knocked from me again. Where the bed should have been, a photo of a waterfall hanging above it, surrounded by pictures of us together, a wall was missing. I stared at the space for a moment, remembering the way that it should have been, then I walked to the edge and looked out. The Sea Shell Moon cast an eerie light onto a vast and dense forest and in the distance I could see a twisting ribbon of light, meandering across the landscape, twinkling in time with the moon. It was too much. I fell to the floor almost sobbing. My mind raced: *Where was I? What was happening? Was I going mad?* In the midst of questioning my own sanity, I heard a noise coming from downstairs. I was not alone after all.

CHAPTER 10

Katie Meister

COMMUNICATION GAP

The giant megaphone was grabbed by the young man and hoisted onto his shoulder.

"Hey, listen up everybody, I'm here and I want to be noticed."

The passers-by just stared as he continued reciting his litany of desires for the people.

"I'm somebody," he said proudly. "I matter and so do you. Don't let people silence your voices. This country is based on the idea that all men are created equal. And that includes you women too. If you came from England, France, Germany, Africa, Ireland, Scotland, Arabia, China, Japan, Russia, or India, it doesn't matter. We don't care. We are all equal. We are Americans and we all have the same rights as each other. Everyone works and pays taxes to keep this country going. We all have the same opportunities for education. If you don't agree, you can say that out loud. If you don't like your life, you can change it. Stand up and be counted. Honor the founders of this country. They lead a rebellion and it worked. They did it for us. US!"

The young man's father rushed over and whisked the megaphone from his son's hand. In broken English and a sheepish voice he told the gathering crowd, "I'm sorry. He's only twelve."

Dear CJ,

Well, I'm back in Iraq for my second tour. When Stephanie and I got married last month, we figured that I would be coming home just after her graduation. Gina met Stephanie when we saw each other in San Diego. We saw her when she was on her way back from her second tour. Gina was mad that we didn't wait 'till she got back, but was ok with it when I told her that no one in the family was there. She's looking forward to getting back to the farm to visit, but she wasn't sure when. When she gets there, she has pictures of Steph and me at the base. She's sure Dad will like Stephanie, so I'm glad we saw her.

The guys here call me the expert cause I was able to fix one of the jeeps that was loaded with shrapnel. I guess I should thank Dad for making us work on all those tractors. By the way, tell dad to send more honey.
AJ

Hey AJ,

I told dad to send honey, and mom to send jam. The strawberry crop was huge this year, so she had me helping with the canning. Dad finally built the laundry room on the back of the house. This is the third laundry room. You still have to go outside, but now it's a covered room. I don't have to get wet bringing my laundry inside anymore. I don't know how Mom did it so long. Dad is using the empty space on the porch to expand his hives. We've got a new bull, and 2 cows are pregnant. I helped build a fence to separate the old bull out. Dad dug another tank and a canal between the two. Dad told me he'd slaughter only one cow this year cause he wants the herd to get bigger. I don't really like my job at the hardware store, but at least it's money. I'd work on the farm all day if it supported me. Stay safe,   CJ

Hey back…

**I said that to one of the guys here and he said, "Hay is for horses,"
back to me. So we all call him Hay now. Well, I did it again. I got an engine to work that was written off. But I had to use my own time for it cause we're so busy. We have another company with us now, but no more**

mechanics. We're near a village, but we aren't near any fighting. This part of the country is pretty calm.

You're just like Dad. He told me to stay safe in his last letter. Has he even used the computer we bought for him yet? I still get his letters from snail mail. You need to teach him how. He taught us stuff we didn't think we would need.

Thanks for the jam and honey. A lot of it went to the kids in the village. It was like Christmas for them, so keep it coming. I traded some with a woman for homemade bread. But the bread here is not like Mom's. I really miss that. The bread here is flat and pretty hard.

I get the best care packages from home, especially if Mom packs them. The whole unit knows when one arrives from Mom. I'm sending you the address of one of the guys who just left. He never had fresh honey until he had some of Dad's. I want you to send him a jar. The guys don't believe that I grew up in a house Dad built, so can you send photos? I also want to see what the new room looks like.   AJ

AJ;

We got a call from Henry Schmidt. He's the new AP at the high school. There's a Giddings High reunion next week and he's hoping there'll be some people from our class there. He has seven confirmed. I told him you weren't around. But I gave him your email address. They want the number to figure out how much meat to barbeque. Mom said she could make some potato salad for me to take. I heard there'd be about 200 people there from 9 graduating classes. Gina's was coming back for it, but she's staying in Austin. She heard that I took her room so she decided to stay with her friends. I told her she could have the upstairs. She said that would be too much like a storage room. I think it is just one friend, and it is probably a guy. Mom would go nuts. I know one guy from her school in Houston works at the capitol building. She's taking Mom and Dad out to dinner for their 35th anniversary while she's here. It will be good for them to get out.

The capitol bats were in the news again. The Giddings newspaper said that the bat population has hit about 7 thousand and some group wants to clear them out from under the bridge. I think the bats should clear that group out. Not much else is going on. Write when you get a chance. CJ

CJ;

Tell Dad he can give a home to some of those bats in the old laundry room next to the hen house. Bats don't eat hens, so that shouldn't be a problem. If anyone brings any petitions around, only sign the ones that let the bats keep their home. Sign my name too; no one'll know the difference. Some of the guys here even knew about the Austin bat bridge. One guy has been there. He said there were hundreds of people just sitting on the side of the hill waiting for dusk. He said that you hear the bats before you see them, and it's really eerie. The weirdest part was that the Capitol Cops just stood around as they watched people drinking beer. He saw a person leave a beer can on the ground and get a ticket for that, but the guy who got in his car just took off. I don't see the problem there. When I get home, we should go into the city and check out the bats. Stephanie would like that. She doesn't believe me that we had cows less than 50 miles from the state capitol building. Maybe Gina can meet us there.

Speaking of bats, whatever became of the flying squirrels? Last time I was home you said they were loose, but keep showing up when they're hungry. That's another thing people don't believe…that I kept a flying squirrel in my bedroom. The cows they believe, so why not a squirrel? Some of these people have really led sheltered lives. Tell Gina I said hi when you see her at the reunion. AJ

I ATE TOO MUCH

Oh my gosh, I ate too much.
I only nibbled
On the Brie and crackers.
I had to have them
To soak up the dry Sauvignon Blanc.
I had no idea we would feast tonight,
So I enjoyed a smidgen of the escargot
And the eggplant puffs.
I naturally followed it with Chardonnay.

We were served wild mushroom soup.
It was delectable.
I'm glad I did not know what was in it
Before I enjoyed it.
I finished my wine just as a new,
Finely etched glass was set in from of me.
As if by magic,
It was filled with a crisp pink Pinot Gris.

I sat in awe
Of the spectacular presentation
Of salmon almandine paired
With wild rice stuffed in artichoke hearts.
I knew it was my duty to be polite
And eat it all.
I was ready to burst
When the chocolate mousse
With raspberry glaze made an appearance.
Oh my gosh, I ate it all.

You Gotta Be Kidding

"You don't really expect me to live here," Gina cried as her dad pulled his rusty old Chevy over the cattle gate and onto his homestead. For as long as she could recall, her father drove out to "the farm" on weekends. He worked on his tractors, planted cotton and vegetables, dug out the fish tank and stocked it with catfish. They were good eating.

Gina had been to the farm once before, but this was the first she knew about her parents' plan to move out here permanently. She had met Leon, the old geezer who owned the peanut farm across the way. Leon let her look for arrowheads in the field after his harvest was in. He also had the closest indoor bathroom. She even helped choose the first cow they owned when Dad took her to the livestock show and rodeo. She had named him Supper, not knowing how prophetic that name would be. But moving to this one-horse town in the middle of nowhere was not on her agenda.

"Dad, you can't do this to me. I'll be a senior this year. You don't know how important that is. I can't leave my friends," Gina wailed.

"We're only a short drive from Austin, and a couple of hours from Houston. You can drive back to see your friends anytime. Even better, your friends can visit out here."

Like that was ever going to happen, Gina thought.

"Giddings has a perfectly good high school. You can be a senior there. You'll probably be at the top of your class," her dad replied, hoping his calm demeanor and positive attitude would help.

"I'm already at the top of my class. The one back in Houston, where I think we should stay for another year."

"Once you get used to it, you'll like it," Dad assured his daughter. He put his arm around her shoulders as they entered the house.

"You really don't get it, Dad. Everyone I know is in Houston. Besides, this building isn't even big enough for all of us to live in." Gina stared at the yellowing masking tape on the floor where it looked like walls belonged. She remembered when her dad had first shown the house to her. The rooms he outlined looked much bigger then. Would there even be enough room for all her clothes? What about her TV set? Then Gina realized, there were no outlets in her room. Was there even enough electricity here to turn on a TV set, much less a hairdryer? At least there were overhead lights, she sighed.

"Come over here and see the kitchen," Dad called to Gina. He didn't have to call loudly; there was only one wall between them. That must be the kitchen and bathroom. Gina sidled up to her dad, screwed up her face, and asked, "What kitchen?"

"The sink will be here in the center of the room, and these two by fours are just temporary, but they will work as counters for now. They support enough cabinets for dishes and pans. The space behind you is where the stove and refrigerator will go. Mom's jam jars and my honey collecting equipment will be stored out on the porch in the pantry I built."

Gina heard the words, but could not see the picture. Mom had more pans and dishes in one cabinet at home than would ever fit in these insignificant cabinets. Mom had a gourmet stove and refrigerator, and they certainly wouldn't fit into the space allotted. The pipe snaking in through the window, above what Dad said was the sink, was connected to the pump outside. What were they supposed to do? Go outside and pump water to do the dishes? Gina decided that wasn't a subject she was going to broach. Her younger brothers did the dishes. That was when she realized something else was missing.

"Dad, we do have indoor plumbing, don't we?" Gina shrieked.

"Well, not yet, but you know where the outhouse is. I'll have an indoor toilet installed for you girls before the winter comes."

Yes. She remembered well where the outhouse was. Depending on the urgency of the need, it was under the barbed-wire fence and across the cow pasture or a dash to the gate a football field away. This farm was a great arrangement for a weekend campout, but not for a girl getting ready for the first day at a new school. Gina saw the satisfied smile on her dad's face and realized that this was his dream. She knew she had to go along this time. She would live here, but she didn't have to like it.

CHAPTER 11

April Lewis

I AM FROM...

I am from the land of lakes
Walled Lake, Duck Lake
Trees, ponds, and wooded areas
Nautical themes is where I hide
Neighbors and friends by my side

I am from Tom and Ellie Lewis
The vines intertwine with Bridget and Derek Marshall
Tangling with Bridget and Derek's little ones
JT, Taryn, and Brendan
Meshed with Shawn my true love
Woven in with a mixture of good friends
All continue to help my candle shine

I am from dealing with the darkness of death
Yet the showering knowledge of an afterlife lingers
Not discouraged by family separation
Enlightened by the human heart
Days of gloom caused by individuals' early demise
Grandparents, Brian, aunts, pets, Tim, a student, and many more relatives
Holding onto hope and promise of the continued love after we pass

I am from unbelievable achievements
Graduating from MSU both undergrad and masters
Gaining knowledge from substituting
To achieving the blessing with South Lyon Schools
Reaching goals and attaining dreams
Meeting Steve Yzerman, traveling to Hawaii, Florida, and much more
Fulfilled with the laughter from my niece and nephews
Sustained by beautiful relationships
Swept away by a boating retreat
Astonished by all of the students I meet
Touched by the music I hear

I am a stuffed taco
A spaghetti meal with wine
Dripping, mouthwatering Cherry Garcia
Grandma's peanut butter cookies
A hamburger not holding anything back
The sweetness of a ripe strawberry.

APRIL

Smiling, Energetic, Analytical, Spontaneous
Aunt of JT, Taryn, and Brendan
Loves family, Shawn, and traveling
Fears death of loved ones, bad dreams, and failing
Desiring to experience Australia, my parents with my future children,
my dad walking me down
the isle
Wild child of the 70's
Lewis

CONTEMPLATION

I'd like to save starving children,
Children who have no place to call home,
Starvation of mind and soul,
Tragedy from abandonment,
Sadness from loss,
Emptiness from unfulfilled dreams,
Hardships that transcend on us all,
Soul-searching,
What can be done?
Watching, listening, feeling,
Analyzing,
Why is it this way?
DISCOVERY
Reaching out a helping hand!

BRIAN'S SPIRIT

His presence was always known,
His spirit glowed, making friends aware they were not alone,
A thunderous, "Dude, what's going on?" let me know he was near,
Feeling when he was around there was nothing to fear.

Brian was his name given to him by his parents,
Hog was his name given to him by his pals,
Bringing complete strangers together
to become best friends is what he did,
Walking people home from parties
to make sure they were safe is why he was treasured.
Hog would drop everything
to help someone, while others just hid.

Hog caused people to bust out into laughter,
Making people smile was his specialty.
He was someone who walked
around an apartment complex aimlessly,
shouting my name
because he didn't know my apartment number.

Agriculture and Design was what he loved,
Flannel shirts were what he wore,
Sharing himself with others was what his life seemed to be for.
Hog—Brian is someone who will always be remembered,
Giving his heart to every individual he came into contact with,
Hog's death is a loss that will continue to be felt by many.

ODE TO WRITING

The words swiftly race through my mind,
Pick me, Pick me!
Captivating images swirling,
Anxiously awaiting the moment
of the sharpened pencil on the crisp white page,
Magical experience,
Heart rushing, mind taunting, tear jerking, exhilarating,
Writing
Embracing,
Visually vibrant images rushing to the page,
Inspiring realizations,
Anxiety
Waiting, contemplating, pacing
Capture it!
Focus!
Relive it!

CHAPTER 12

Mary Cox

ROLLER COASTER RELATIONSHIP

Swirling bubbles of hilarity catch in my throat.
Slowly I rise.

Gravity pulls me back with each shaky click of the cross tie.

Pressed back

For a moment facing only the wide open space of sunbeam and ether,
Feeling empathy with those creatures that populate this space.

Ah, I could adore the god who brought me to this pinnacle.

I could stay suspended between earth and sky

Free

But the moment passes,
The fulcrum shifts
And there is a crushing rush back to the mundane.

I Met Someone Today

Today, I met someone who knows you.

The mention of your name was like pulling off the scab on an old wound
Expecting to find healthy, shiny, pink skin;
Instead finding writhing maggots
Of hurt, anger, lies and loss.

How could I not have sensed this infection and fever
Raging through my body
Masquerading as "getting over you"?

Today I met someone who knows you
And we compared scars.

SMALL MOMENTS TO SAVE

That moment at dawn
When the sky changes from night to light
And becomes day

The moment of watching a drop of rain
Hanging on the leaf
And containing the whole world

That instant the sun touches the horizon
Creating a bridge of orange
From me to eternity

CHAPTER 13

John Callaghan

LETTER POEM

Inspired by an exercise in
Getting the Knack
By Stephen Dunning and
William Stafford
(NCTE, 1992)
July 15, 2007

Dear Roy Rogers,

You and Trigger are long dead.
I am writing this because
I still haven't forgiven you for what
You did to me on a December morning,
1947, in Detroit Hudson's dining room.

I am just-turned-eight and have seen
All your movies,
You conquering evil in every one of them,
And there you are sitting at that table,
Roped off, with Dale glittering next to you-
You, with that huge 10-gallon hat,

Face deeply tanned and burnished
Like a well traveled, leather saddle.

We are Christmas shopping, me and Mom, and
Just by chance in the flesh, sitting there eating breakfast
Is my hero, not in gritty, filmy black and white
But in *living* color!

My joy tears me away from Mom,
My voice squeaking "It's Roy Rogers!"
I'm leaping over the velvet-roped barrier,
Hoping to sing your praises, to worship the
Real you, in the flesh, in the flesh…
The sneer erupting under that pure white hat
Across that god-like face
Pins me to the floor,
That tenor voice hollering,
Breaking my heart:
"Waiter! Get that brat away from us."

I stand there before my hero's altar,
The goddess Dale frowning in disapproval,
Her pasty makeup caked beneath the spangled
Cowgirl hat,
An eight year old boy, stripped naked before the
Universe of stardom, shocked by rejection,
Regret, remorse, humiliation.

The waiter tugs me away and I know the pain
Will last forever.
A fist to the nose, a kick in the groin, a bitter,
Vomity taste in my mouth.
Enjoy your breakfast and happy trails

To you.

　A former fan,

　John Callaghan

MORNING JUSTICE

I'm not sure what wakes me. One minute I'm asleep. The next minute I'm staring up at a pistol, wondering what in hell that is, knowing full well it's a real pistol, the bullets in the cylinder little lead-gray phalluses ready to spit forth my death. I see behind the gun a clean cut young face staring down the sights at me, the eyes narrow, angry, under a New York State trooper's hat pitched back on his head.

"Don't twitch a muscle, buster, or your brains are on the ground."

"Jesus Christ Jesus..."

That's my friend Buddy Moceri waking up on the other side of the clearing. Believe me, it isn't a prayer. Another state trooper is pointing his .38 police special at Buddy with his right hand; handcuffs dangle from his left.

My trooper hisses at me, "You and your pal enjoy busting into cabins and raping old ladies? She may not live, you prick, and I'd love to see you jump up and make a run for it, you know, resisting arrest, something like that."

I can't believe what he's saying, but his eyes tell me he would like an excuse to empty his gun into my head. I feel like a cockroach caught in the sudden kitchen light. My voice sounds high-pitched, insincere: "Hey, we got lost on this old road last night, couldn't find the old cabin Buddy over there rented from a neighbor back in Oswego. We stopped to wait for daylight so we could find it easier."

"Sure, sure, and that car over there just happens to be a '58 Chevy, the one spotted leaving the area near the old lady's cabin."

I glance over to where he's jerking his head, and I see Buddy's '58 Impala up on the dirt road with the state trooper's car cutting it off at an angle, the rasping sound of a two-way radio coughing out static and an occasional bored metallic message. Maybe that's what woke me up.

I'm glancing back at the muzzle of the gun, and I'm saying, "Hey, there are all kinds of Chevies around... All right, all right. The cabin I'm talking about belongs to Buddy's uncle, but we did get lost last night trying to find the damn thing. Right, Buddy?"

Buddy is staring up at the other trooper, his face gray with shock, nodding yes-yes-yes, but it's to some voice from within. I can't be sure if he hears me or not, but all I can think of is a turtle on its back waiting to be crushed.

"Anyway, we left about 7:30 last night, you know, after work and last minute stuff. We stop to pick up a few beers and some burgers on the way so it took over three hours. Buddy kinda got fuzzy about which is the turnoff to the north end of the lake. The roads and forks got stranger and stranger and it's getting later and later..." And I think, *Drunker and drunker*, but I don't say it. "So we saw this clearing down off the road and said what the hell. It's warm enough. We'll sleep here until sunup and then find the place easier. Right, Bud?"

I'm trying to swallow the ache in my throat, my hands quivering like my voice, my back soaked with fear sweat and morning dew. Out of the corner of my eye I see Buddy is still nodding to his inner voice.

"Bull shit!" The trooper's eyes are slits of disbelief. "Turn over slowly onto your stomach and put your hands behind your back."

The handcuffs chew into my wrists, and my shoulders ache as much as my beery head. Tears sting at my eyelids, and I have a tremendous urge to pee. And I'm thinking, *Please, God, don't let him get gun happy until he finds out the truth.*

"Got the other guy secure, Hal?" My trooper likes yanking on the handcuffs, so I have to do a pushup with my chin to relieve the pressure on my shoulders.

I hear Hal say, "Yep. He doesn't have much to say, does he? Who owns the Chevy?"

"Him," I say and I feel like a little kid tattling on a schoolmate.

In that prone position, I'm trying to nod toward Buddy as best I can. He's on his back, his hands cuffed behind him, and I can see just his forehead and his eyes bugging out of his face in disbelief, out of focus, almost crazed.

My trooper is saying, "Right make, '58 two-tone Chevy, and 'OS2' the first three plate marks, just like the report says. Got so drunk you pass out on the road? Yea, sure. You guys are real winners! Couple of punks robbing an old lady never hurt a soul in her life. Beat the piss out of her and then try to finish her off with a little rape job?"

An obscene vision of my Grandma Hogan flashes through my head, and I have to gulp hard at my heaving stomach.

Trooper Hal says, "What do you think, Jer, my gun just sort of misfiring and shooting this one's balls off, give him another sort of thrill?"

"Naw... not just yet, Hal. Let's make sure first."

I hear a ringing sound in my ears, my head pounding a pulse I'd never felt before.

Hal reaches under Buddy and jerks the cuffs trying to turn him over, and the chinking sound distracts me. Just last night, a few hours ago really, Buddy's grinning at me, shaking his head in resignation, giving me the keys to his Impala: I'd wangled the Saturday morning off so that we could have two nights on the lake. Besides, the trip's my original idea. So I get to drive the "beast," Buddy's pride and joy. At first we're going to borrow a tent, but Buddy checks with his uncle, and no one's using his cabin that weekend. We're all set. A break from the numbing routine of summer work.

I can still see myself driving with one hand on a beer and the gas pedal threatening the floorboard. The big engine is perking, and we're flying down the empty road. Buddy stops complaining about his precious car after the second beer. I can feel the boredom slide out of me as we chew up the miles. We talk about how great it will be to start our junior year at Buffalo U. and get away from the hauling and pulling, the pack animal work, unloading box car after box car of lumber, cement bags, nail kegs, you name it. Our bodies are sore, hands blistered, the skin on our thighs lined with a month's worth of embedded slivers. We even joke about how long it takes each morning to get rid of the previous day's soreness.

I almost go off the road laughing at Buddy's imitation of the old farts at Fuzzy's Bar on a Saturday night when we whip them one after another in arm wrestling for free beers. I do a pretty good imitation of Virgie, a skinny, aging waitress at Ernie's, a twenty-four hour greasy spoon, her voice ever patient even at 3:00 AM, taking breakfast orders from a bunch of beered up slobs, including us.

A female voice squawking over the patrol car's radio brings me back. It replaces the monotone of the male voice we've been hearing just on the periphery of our senses, droning out the usual police stuff. The two troopers recognize the change too and look at each other the way kids do when they're about to argue who's going to do the dishes.

"I'll get it, Jer."

Hal bends over and cups his hands under Buddy's shoulders and jerks and drags him until he is face to face with me on the ground. Buddy's breath hisses out with each jerk, and his eyes flash from fear to annoyance to anger. Buddy and I exchange What-did-we-do-to-deserve-this expressions. Trooper Jer backs up slightly, flexes his knees, and points his pistol between our heads. I can't make out what Hal is saying on the police radio, but the sound of his voice is animated, then anguished; angry, then perplexed. For some reason, he shuts off the patrol car's engine.

"Come over here a sec, will you, Jer? Just let 'em be. They're not going anywhere just now."

Jer pivots away from us in surprise, his hand cupping the trigger guard of the pistol. Buddy looks at me, his eyebrows bunching with worry. "Tom," he whispers, his lips barely moving, "whatever you do, don't let them fool you into running. They'll shoot you as soon as look at you. Our only chance is for them to get us into town--hopefully Plattsburg--and we can call home for help."

"No running for me, Buddy. No way."

"Just do everything they say. I think the Jer guy is a little more cautious than the other one. Maybe we can talk them into taking us in before they try something stupid, and shoot us like, like a couple a cattle rustlers or something."

"Cattle rustlers, Buddy? You've been watching too many of those John Wayne flicks." But my voice cracks and I can't hide the tears. Buddy's voice is strained too.

"They're not killers. It's our only chance."

"We're not killers either."

"I wish they knew that."

We both notice the quiet. No engine. No radio static. No voices. Just chattering birds and insects, ignoring the human intrusion. Footsteps approach, hesitant, reluctant. Jer's voice is pinched, the words recited like a 9th grader's history report.

"The perpetrators have been arrested just south of here, '58 Chevy Impala, two-tone. License plate OSW-339. Probably from around the Oswego area too. Recently released from Auburn after serving five for armed robbery in Syracuse. We apologize for the inconvenience."

Hal is unlocking Buddy's cuffs and helping him up, gently, like a medic with a wounded soldier; Trooper Jer is holstering his pistol and groping for his keys. I push my forehead into the ground, grinding my teeth, gulping at the words of rage foaming up from my throat. Jerry uncuffs me, and I rub my wrists furiously, trying to ignore the ache in my shoulders, not to mention the one in my soul. Buddy has that glare in his eyes, that jut to his jaw I've seen when someone is foolish enough to call him "Dago-Bud" or, worse, "Ginea-Bud"; and then there's no controlling him if he starts swinging. I say, "Don't Bud, it's not worth it." He doesn't hear me until I shout, "Please, Bud! No!"

Jer and Hal startle and make foolish dabs at their holsters. But Buddy hears me, smiling that cold unforgiving smile of his. Hal looks scared but turns his palms up, his hands bobbing for understanding.

"Hey, we're just doing our job, guys. We see the Chevy, you two lying there with the pile of beer cans. What do you expect us to think? We knew the old lady. Jenny Mae Gibson. Gave us cakes and pies ever since we rescued her son from a sorry group of assholes he was hangin' with. Kindest sweetheart you'd ever want to meet. So we're sorry for the mix-up."

Jerry looks at Hal, his eyes glaring Shut-your-mouth-before-you-get-us-into-more-trouble. But then he shrugs and says, "He's right, almost everything matched up. Uh...can we help you find your cabin? It's the least we can do."

I want to say something nasty, but can't think of anything vile enough. Then I notice the rays of the sun stabbing through the tree branches and feel their early morning warmth. It's going to be a clear summer day on Lake

Champlain. I can see the blue-green shimmer of the lake off in the distance. The cabin is probably on the other side of the bay.

But, I think, *I'd rather be at work. It's safer.*

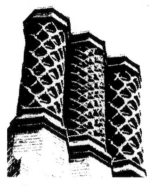

CHAPTER 14

Kathleen Reddy-Butkovich

WINDOW MANUSCRIPT

Sunlight slips a note under the door.
Open the curtains. Look through the glass.
A shimmer of shingles raise rooftops to blue.
Faithful cardinals arrive and watch,
While squirrels like squatters claim the feeder.
Ancient trees pose as ballroom dancers
Casting shadows across the grass.
A stand of Shasta daisies lean together
And gossip in the garden wind.
One black cat sleeps like a comma.
A pause on a transparent page,
That is waiting for response.

CAUTIONARY TALES

Composed in a green chaise lounge
Patio poet

One small chickadee,
Treetop interlocutor,
Heed her warning call.

Snapdragons are slain.
Without water to survive,
Color extinguished.
Oh, hungry squirrel
Demanding human handouts,
Beware of fast food.

THREE NOUNS

At the start of a professional development workshop about writing, teachers pause to notice this Japanese word, "saku-taku-no-ki." It names the moment the sound of a mother hen tapping on the outside of an egg and the baby chick tapping on the inside of the egg reach the same spot. The egg cracks open. New life emerges. This wonderful word is found in *Take Joy--A Book for Writers* (2003). The author, Jane Yolen, makes the connection to writing in this way:

> In just the same way a story begins, with a physical tapping on the outside: a line of a song that won't leave your head, an article in the newspaper that strikes a chord, a fragment of conversation that loops endlessly... a repeating dream. And then the answering emotion that taps within... The moment they come together, the story starts.

It seems that amid all the books, benchmarks, and beliefs about teaching and learning, a small snippet of a presentation by Donald Graves keeps tapping at me. I am in the audience of a large conference session. Donald Graves, Professor Emeritus at the University of New Hampshire and writing researcher for three decades, is standing in the front of the room at an overhead projector, sport coat off, white shirtsleeves rolled up. He is teaching us about "quick writes" and first draft writing. To demonstrate some recent work published in his book, *Inside Writing: How to Teach the Details of Craft* (2005), he is writing along with us. Eventually, we are wrapped in his words and wisdom.

He reminds us of the importance of knowing our students. Graves says, "The more I know a child, the more I can expect of him." We recall that "sea of faces" feeling we have at the start of a new school year. We remember that a classroom community grows by knowing the details of how our students learn, what they want, and what interests them. As Graves continues, he reminisces about a three-column exercise that can help us reflect on our students and our teaching. Try it.

In the first column, write the names of your students from memory. Next, try to place three solid nouns opposite each name—details that characterize experiences and interests of each student. For example, next to Meghan you write new braces, songs, jogger; or next to Danny you write hockey, books, dog trainer. Then put an X in a third column when you can confirm, with specifics, that the child knows what you have observed about her or him. For

103

example, you had a conversation with Meghan about how she chooses a song to perform, or you brought an article about the local hockey team for Danny to read. Later, you might add some verbs, but Graves nudges us again to first represent each student with at least three strong nouns.

Now is a great time to pause, ponder, and write. The more we know our students, the more we can expect of them. Listen.

CHAPTER 15

Ronnelle G. Payne

MIRROR, MIRROR

What's in the mirror, can you see?
Does the mirror really define me?
My hair, my nose, my lips, my eyes
Tell me, why do you criticize?

What do these things show?
The real me, do you know?
Tell me, what do you see?
I am content to just let it be.

For you see, the mirror does not define me.
My face, my clothes are not my personality.
Inside me does the truth really lie.
My soul, my spirit—mirrors of God's eyes.

Genesis 1:27 NIrV

So God created human beings in his own likeness.
He created them in the likeness of God.
He created them as male and female.

GOD'S ANSWER TO MIRROR, MIRROR

The mirror, my daughter, can't you see
is an object; it cannot define thee.
In my image and likeness as such
your inner beauty, a mirror cannot touch.

Formed from my hands to shape and mold
poured in my spirit to behold.
Gifted, talented, after my own heart
vessels of love through every part.
To rule over all the earth
have I deemed thee.
Your breath of life
comes only from me.
There is but one mirror
to which you can account.
Your glistening beauty
as radiant as a fount.

My eyes upon thee will I bestow.
Your essence,
from the mirror of my eyes
to the world you will show.

THE *ME* SYMPHONY

Each note, each measure
My Symphony

Who am I to be?
What I hear leads me
What does the Creator want of me?
Let Him conduct my symphony?

Each key,
Each chord,
The rests,
The rhythm

What does He want me to be?

Direct those melodies upon my heart

Lord, let me be you instrument
Compose my symphony.

Tandem

"Why won't you talk to me?"
I write you letters. I pour out my heart in those letters.
Not fearful.
Not intimidated.
Does that mean I don't communicate?
I communicate—just on a different venue!
You think there's something wrong with me.
There isn't.
I just rather write to you.
I love writing.
I like the flow of the pen, the language, the words, the letters connected with continuous curves and loops.
Writing is simply beautiful. I can express myself clearly and succinctly.
No, there's no problem.
Everything I could say in the written word could absolutely be conveyed verbally.
Yeah, I could do that—I just choose not to!

We argue every time I hand you one of my letters.
Obviously I want to express myself.
It's the highlight of my day, choosing pages from my adolescent stationary, carefully selecting the right pen—not medium point.
I haven't graduated to fine point yet—oh, the felt tip.
The flow of the ink as it glides along the page.

DON'T YOU GET IT?

You refuse to read another letter.
"Why won't you talk to me?" you ask.
"I just don't."

I think I write beautifully.
I practice and practice and practice my handwriting. How do you make your F's? Can I really get your flow down?
Each letter is in perfect measure, equidistant.

I'm trying to imitate your personality
I see in your writing.

Don't hold my writing against me.
Don't stifle me.
I don't have the letter disease.
I talk when I have something to say, trust me.
I'm my own person.

I guess my letters are foreplay—the catalyst for our discussions.

"Talk to me."

"I do.

"No Que Pasa Aquí

Fill out the application in its entirety,
you say to me
And, although it's optional to check your ethnicity,
the government keeps track of these demographics
to improve services, you see
White,
Black,
Native American,
Asian,
Hispanic,
Of course

But, what the hell is this?

Hispanic-Latino,
Hispanic-Black
        No remorse
So, if I check Hispanic-Black
am I a double minority?
Do I now qualify for double benefits
for my family?

In a race already categorized a minority
Are you causing yet another divide within my nationality?
What purpose?
What reason?
do you give
For the racism you spread,
but keep hid.
That Willie Lynch shit
Divide and conquer,
"House nigga"
"Field nigga"
"House spic"
"Field spic"
No que pasa aquí

Spain, Mexico, South America

What do we do?

What are you trying to prove?

Check "other."

    Fuck you!

CHAPTER 16

Bonnie Cates

I AM FROM...

I am from tender turnip greens and sweet ice tea
I am from pinto beans
and hot corn bread
with smooth, freshly churned butter.
I am from Grace and Bonnie

I'm from church every Sunday because
"they'll be no heathens in this family"
I'm from Grandma's aluminum Christmas tree
with the three colored light wheel
and the smell of Grandpa's cherry cigars filling the air
as I run through the house with the band on my finger.

I am from having breakfast with
Milky the Clown and Captain Kangaroo,
Lunch with Soupy Sales and
Dinner with Mickey Mouse,
Howdy Doody, and the Peanut Gallery
I am from fighting my brother and sister
for a good spot in front of the little TV

I'm from sitting on bleachers for hours
in the blazing hot sun, chilling rain,
and freezing snow,
being a soccer, baseball, basketball, football,
and cheerleader mom.
I am from sitting front row center
as a proud thespian mom
and an Air Force mom sitting proudly
as my son marches onto the field. .

I am from sitting proudly with bouquets of flowers,
through dance recitals and cheerleading practices.
I am from crying when I first saw my daughter
in her wedding gown
And proud, happy, and scared, as my lovely daughter
gave birth to my beautiful grandson and grand daughter

I am from being a gleam in my father's eye,
a daughter, granddaughter, sister, aunt,
wife, mother and now
a Granny.

WILL

Cute, cuddly, happy, energetic,
Big brother of his little sister
Who loves to play in the pool, swing on his swing,
and make beauteous music
Who is afraid of loud noises, the vacuum, and not much else
Who wants to see; bubbles floating in the air,
the birds, squirrels, chipmunks, and rabbits
playing outside, and everything else there is to see
Wild child of the future

Lee

GRANDSON

Little William Lee
Granny's cutie patoutie,
And mommy's wild child.

GRANDDAUGHTER

Jessica, tiny baby girl
Granny's precious little princess
And mommy's sweetheart.

ROCKY
Cuddly, chubby
Stalking, purring, sleeping
He's a cat that loved to eat Cheetos and whip cream.
Pooh

ON TOP OF THE WORLD

Looking out at the blue sky and white, puffy clouds, I wonder if these are cumulus or cirrus; are those types of clouds? I used to know, but that was a long time ago, probably in seventh grade. Anyway, the clouds dot the sky moving ever so slowly to the east. I wonder how long it will take them to get to Port Huron.

I wonder if these are the some of the same clouds my son saw about three days ago, as he looked up at the sky when he came out of one of the missile silos at the Minot, North Dakota, Air Force Base.

I know it's the same sun and moon we both see, and I know that the weather he sees today I'll be seeing in about three days

So, why not the clouds? Or are these new clouds that were formed as the winds blew over Lake Michigan?

No, I like to think these are the same clouds, another link to the son I love and miss so much.

SILVER AND GOLD

Natasha, Max, and Gus, her cats, jump up on the bed, meowing and walking all over her, telling her it's time to get up. So another day begins. She goes through her morning routine of getting up, getting dressed in her comfy clothes, making a pot of tea, and feeding the dogs and cats. She puts a little honey in her cup of tea, and goes out on the deck. She quietly snuggles up, on the swing; in the quilt her grandmother made her so many years ago. It's a beautiful morning. The sun is just peeking over the pine trees at the east end of the lake. The icy blue water is quiet and serene, the calm before the storm. Soon the glassy lake would be filled with loud boats, skiers, and boisterous Ski-Doos.

But six o'clock in the morning is her time to just sit and think and enjoy nature. Just her and the early morning robins and sparrows chirping to be first to eat at the overly full bird feeder in the tall oak tree, and the tiny quick hummingbird poking her beak in and out of the small purple flowers of the huge blue potato bush nearby.

Out of the corner of her eye she sees Chip and Dale, the two little brown chipmunks, race out of the safety of the tall wild grass that grows on the side of the yard. They're racing to be first to get to the scrumptious feeding tray. Today they're in for a surprise; a nice, juicy apple is waiting for them.

Life is good, and she enjoys this quiet morning time. Just sitting, thinking, reminiscing, sometimes she wishes, just once, this could last all day, but not today. After quietly getting another cup of tea, she settles back and just swings. It's already 6:45, but there's still time to sit and swing.

She sees Donald and Daisy Duck taking the kids for a walk down to the lake for an early morning swimming lesson and breakfast. Greta and George Goose and their four goslings swim up to the shore to see what nature may have left them to munch for breakfast, and after not finding much in the way of nourishment, they move on down the lake.

All of a sudden she hears tiny voices in the house. It's already five to eight. She feels the warmth of the sun as she takes one more look at the beautiful morning nature has given her. She picks up her cup and finishes her tea. While still wrapped in her quilt, she slowly gets out of the swing, and heads for the door. As she opens it, she hears tiny footsteps running down the hall.

119

"Let's go find granny!" and childish laughter suddenly fills the air and she sees her daughter, grandson, and granddaughter with big smiles on their faces, coming into the kitchen. Big hugs and "Is breakfast ready yet?" is music to her ears.

She knows this is what life is all about. Remembering past times can be great, but the now time is where life's really at.

So, with her family and friends, she keeps making new memories, as she keeps the old,

One is silver and the other is gold.

THINGS TO SAVE (CORINNE)

I'd like to save the moment I found out I was pregnant with my first child
When I discovered it was a girl
I'd like to save the moment I first felt her move inside me
When I first heard her little heartbeat
I'd like to save the moment I first saw and held her in my arms
My daughter, my own
I'd like to save the moment she said her first words and took her first steps
Her red sequined costume for her first dance recital
I'd like to save the moment she became a princess and was mesmerized at the
sight of Cinderella's Castle in Disney World
I'd like to save the moment she stepped up to get her high school and college
diplomas
I'd like to save the moment I first saw her in her wedding dress
And walked her down the aisle to the man she loves and who loves her
I'd like to save the moment I first found out I was going to be a
grandmother
When I first saw his picture and heard his heartbeat
I'd like to save the moment when my daughter became a mother
And I became a Granny.

THINGS TO SAVE (DENNIS)

I'd like to save the moment I found out I was pregnant with my second child
When I discovered it was a boy
I'd like to save the moment I first felt him move inside me
When I first heard his little heartbeat

I'd like to save the moment I first saw and held him in my arms
My son, my own
I'd like to save the moment he said his first words and took his first steps
Then his first steps to kindergarten, soccer, baseball, karate, basketball and football
I'd like to save the moment I first saw him, as a thespian, up on the stage, in his first musical, singing and dancing, and then on to many more performances
I'd like to save the moments of both of us 'skipping' school, sitting together at the movies, eating popcorn, and watching the first showing of all the "Star Wars and Star Trek" movies
I'd like to save the moment I saw him in his tux for the prom and sat proudly in the stands, watching, as he received his high school diploma
I'd like to save the moment he told me he was joining the Air Force
Then watching him get on that plane, bravely going to serve his country
I'd like to save that sunny morning in San Antonio, Texas, sitting in the stands, looking over the sea of men and women for a glimpse of my son
I'd like to save the moment he became an Airman in the United States Air Force
And I sat proudly watching.

CHARLIE'S TALE

It looked as if it were going to be a dark and stormy night, and the five friends were sitting around the camp talking about their day and wondering where Charlie might be.

"It's not like him to be out this late," said Joe.

"Well, we saw Charlie about six o'clock this morning while we were out in the field, but not since," Mike and Jenny said.

Bob, Katie and Joe hadn't seen him at all.

Then Bob added, "Charlie's been cruising these woods for a lot of years; he'll be here soon, you can bet on it."

As the friends were all hoping that nothing had happened to their friend, they suddenly heard rustling in the bushes just outside the camp. Apprehensively, they looked out into the darkness and saw Charlie come sauntering in.

"Hey, guys! How you doing? Did you miss me?" Charlie joked.

"Charlie, where have you been? We've all been worried about you. You know, it's not safe to be out late this time of year," his friends answered back.

"Oh, no problem, sorry to worry all of you though, but wait till you hear about my day," Charlie said.

Everyone settled in and Charlie began his tale.

"Well, as you know the morning was cold and crisp and I knew I'd better get up. It was still dark, probably only about five o'clock, but you know what they say, 'The early deer gets the best grass and maybe sugar beets and carrots.' So I slowly stretched out my legs and got to my hooves. Gave another stretch, looked to see if the neighbors were up yet. I didn't see any of you guys, so I ventured out to find breakfast, before the sun came up. As I wandered down my usual path, nibbling a little grass here and there, I saw two figures out in the old cornfield. I thought about joining them but then noticed it was Mike and Jenny, and you know what they say, 'Two's company and three's a crowd.'"

Rumor has it that they got a 'thing going on,' and I didn't want to interrupt anything, so I moseyed on through the woods. "

Mike looked at Jenny and she blushed.

"As I got near the big oak tree, you know the one on the edge of the open field? Well, I noticed a new, different smell in the air. I'm not sure what it was. It smelled a little like a man scent, but there was something more, kind of a flowery smell, but there aren't any flowers around this time of year. So, you know, I was even more on my guard. As I cautiously walked on, the smell got stronger. I stopped and listened. At first I didn't hear anything. But then a tiny rustling came from above. I looked up, and you guys are never going to believe what I saw. I'm telling you it was really unbelievable. I mean, I saw it and I can hardly believe it myself," he said.

"Well, do we have to guess, or are you planning on telling us, some time tonight?" kidded Joe.

Charlie continued, "Sure, well, like I said I looked up, and there in the tree was a man. At least I think it was a man. But unlike any man I have ever seen, and believe me I have seen a lot of them in my years. Anyway, this man was all orange. I mean from head to hoof. It was the brightest orange I had ever seen, but one thing was different. The man smelled nice. I mean, just like the wild flowers that grow in the clearing in the spring. So I think it must have been a girl-man. "

"I like the smell of the wild flowers in the spring," Katie and Jenny chimed in.

"Well anyway, she was sitting up in the tree, and I don't think she really was **too** smart because if she was trying to hide—puleese—an orange creature, sitting in a brown tree, with bare branches? Ha, ha. I could see her a mile away. So I went up for a closer look. Even though I was really quiet, she must have heard me because she looked down and saw me--I mean we were looking eye to eye. But she didn't have brown eyes like us; she had beautiful blue eyes like the color of the lake or the sky on a beautiful summer day. I wonder what I would look like with blue eyes. What do you think?" asked Charlie.

"Yeah right, Charlie, you with blue eyes! Ha, ha," said Bob.

"I think Charlie would look scrumptious with eyes the color of the sky," cooed Katie.

"Ooooo, Katie and Charlie, sitting by the tree, k-i-s-s-i-n-g," chimed in the other deer.

"Ha, ha! You guys are just jealous," Charlie winked at Katie. "Anyway she looked down at me, and I looked up at her for about a minute, and I knew I didn't have anything to fear from her. There was a nice look in those eyes. All of a sudden she started fumbling around up there again and pointed a thing at me. It was the same shape as the salt lick."

"Oh, Charlie, you could have been killed," cried Katie.

"No, it wasn't a dangerous kind of thing," he said. "She wasn't that kind of girl-man. She just pointed the thing at me. I looked at it and her, gave a little wink and a smile. I heard a couple of clicks; then I turned, rubbed my antlers a little on the side of the tree, and walked away, leaving the orange girl-man up there."

"Wow, Charlie you are so lucky," said Mike

"Oooo, and so brave, too," chimed in Jenny and Katie.

"Careful, is more like it. Anyway, I still hadn't had breakfast, and I was hoping there would be some of those sweet, sugar beets lying around by the clearing. I walked on down. Found enough grass and beets to fill my belly, and then I found a safe place in the field to lie down for the rest of the day. I must have been really tired because I didn't wake up until I heard the thunder just a little while ago. And yadda, yadda, yadda, here I am. Hey, I've been hogging all the conversation. How about you guys? How was your day?" asked Charlie.

"Nothing like yours, Charlie, none of us saw any men in the woods today, and here's hoping we don't run into any of them for the rest of the season," whispered Bob, Mike and Joe.

Just then they heard another crack of thunder and saw a bolt of lightning flash in the sky, and it definitely became a dark and stormy night. So the deer retreated to their beds and as Charlie snuggled up with Katie, he had one last thought and chuckle about the nice smelling big orange girl-man 'hiding' up in the old oak tree.

ORANGE-GIRL'S STORY

I have to admit I was pretty excited to be getting away even for a few days. I hadn't gone on vacation that summer. I had just lounged around the pool, and summer is always over much too soon. So when my friends asked me to join them up at the cabin, I jumped at the opportunity. We were going up November thirteenth, right after work, and we'd be gone five days. It was going to be a nice little get away; I took a couple new books and planned on just sitting around, reading books and not doing much of anything else.

It was about a three hour drive, and when we got to the cabin, we were all exhausted and looking forward to the next few days. My friends were going hunting, and I was planning on snuggling in a comfy chair, drinking a few mugs of tea, and catching up on my reading.

After a good night's sleep, we were up early Friday morning, had breakfast, and then everyone was off to make sure their blinds were cleaned up, straightened up, or patched up, readied for opening day on the fifteenth. I wandered around here and there in the woods, with the 'hunters' helping. But I really couldn't understand how these people I knew would want to get up in the middle of the night, freezing cold outside, bundle up and go sit in a tree or on the ground for hours, waiting for a deer to come along and then shoot it.

I was the only novice in the group. I hadn't ever shot a gun. But after cleaning things up in the woods, everyone went back to the cabin to get their rifles ready, making sure they had ammo and that their scopes were sighted. They had pyramids of beer cans and bowling pins set up to shoot at, and as I sat and watched them practice, I must admit I became curious about shooting. I was easily coerced into just trying it once. I was scared at first to handle the gun, but after shooting off a few rounds, I surprisingly became more at ease with it. In fact, when I hit one of the beer cans, I excitedly twirled around with the rifle in my hands, shouting happily, "I hit it, I hit it!" while the rest of the group flopped to the ground and said, "Stop! Put the gun down. Put the gun down." That was when I found out you are not supposed to spin around with a loaded gun in your hands. Imagine that.

Well, even though I was just shooting at cans and bowling pins, the power of the gun and the shooting began to exhilarate me. The weapon empowered me, and I could understand the 'rush' shooters talk about. To this day I'm not sure if I felt it as a good rush or not, but I definitely got sucked into shooting and eventually even going hunting. I knew in my heart I could never shoot another living animal, but with the insistence of my friends and the high I was on, I agreed to join them on their hunting expedition the next day.

Now as a novice there are certain rules my 'good friends' made sure I was aware of:

- Number 1 - as a hunter you are not allowed to turn around in your blind. You have a one hundred eighty degree radius and that's it.
- Number 2 - you have to be quiet when you're out in the woods.
- Number 3 - the new guy is not allowed to come down from the tree until the 'hunters' come back to get them, so don't drink too much in the morning.
- Number 4 - make sure you dress in layers because while it may be very cold in the morning, as the sun comes up it gets a little warmer.
- Number 5 - and last but not least, the most important thing: the new guy has to sit in the tree and wear the bright orange hunting outfit, including the orange hat.

So everyone else had on the 'camouflage outfit' with an orange hat because they're on the ground behind me and I had to make sure I followed the above five rules. I must admit that night when I crawled into bed I was feeling pretty geeked about opening day. The alarm went off at about four thirty a. m. I got up, showered with my sweetpea shower gel, got dressed in layers, put on my big orange pants, jacket, gloves, boots, and hat. I looked like a giant pumpkin; it was all my friends could do to keep from laughing their heads off.

It was almost five o'clock, and in hunting time this was pretty late, so we all started off for the woods. I was the first one they dropped off. In my big electric orange hunting suit, rifle in hand, book and bottle of water in my pocket and camera hanging around my neck, I climbed up the big oak tree. What a sight that must have been from behind, I can only imagine. There was a stool up there, so I sat down, put my bottle of water beside me, and was reminded of rule number one – only shoot in front, remember a one hundred eighty degree radius because everyone else was behind me in the woods.

Since it was still dark, I couldn't read my book yet, so I just sat and enjoyed the early morning and the eventual sunrise. As I sat with the gun across my lap, I knew in my heart that I would never be able to point the gun at a living creature and pull the trigger. But I sat in the tree anyway, hands on the rifle, and waited. I thought of what my friends had assured me: that just like the rush I felt as I was shooting at the cans, when I saw a deer I'd be able to aim, shoot and kill it. This wasn't me, but now maybe because I wanted to fit in, I was willing to go along with all the joking and kidding and actually contemplate killing an animal.

I remembered quite a few years ago when I accidentally ran over a squirrel on the road, I had to pull over because I was so upset. When my kids' pets died, even the iguana, I cried. How could I let myself be talked into this? I just wanted to be part of the group. After all, these were my friends, we had traveled and done things together, and now I was hunting with them.

Oh, the things we do to try to fit in! Even though I knew in my heart it might be okay for my friends, it was not okay for me to be following them. So I put the gun down on the floor of the tree stand, sat, and waited for the sun to come up.

I sat and waited and sat and thought and just sat watching, enjoying the sunrise. It was soon light enough to read and take a few pictures. It was beautiful up there. I'm not sure how long I sat, but not long after sunrise I heard a rustling in the woods behind me. Since I no longer had the gun, I knew I could peek around the back of the tree. Maybe it was my friends coming back to get me. But no, hunters stay in the woods until about noon. Deer are usually on the move from just before dawn to around noon, as I was told. As I sat back down I heard the rustling again. I sat quietly and then out of the shadows walked one of the most beautiful animals I had ever seen. He was majestic, his smooth brown fur with just a hint of white around the collar and on his chest, and a rack with at least ten points.

The buck looked around the clearing, gave a few snorts. [Man was he loud!] He looked up. I looked down. We were looking face to face. He had the softest brown eyes I had ever seen, so cautious and yet so trusting. I just sat there in awe of this beautiful animal. I finally got my wits about me and quietly took my gloves off so I wouldn't scare him away, and got my camera ready to take a picture. The funny thing is, he just looked up at the camera and me. When I clicked off a few pictures, he just stood there looking at me. Then he shook his head a little, rubbed his antlers on the side of the tree and turned and walked away. I just sat watching him, white tail bobbing, in front of me. I was glad he didn't walk behind me because I knew what was waiting for him back there, and I didn't want 'my deer' being shot that day.

When my friends finally came back to get me, I had been sitting in that tree about five hours, during which time I picked up the gun only to take the bullets out and set it back down. Climbing out of the tree, I heard disappointment from my friends because they hadn't seen anything all day. When asked, I told them I saw a buck. They commented they didn't hear any shots. I told them I couldn't shoot it and handed over the gun and bullets. Of course they razzed me, as they had about the wearing of the orange, but I didn't care. Later I showed them my pictures and their comments made me sad again because if they had him in their sights, he would have been hanging on the tree out back of the cabin.

The next few days were uneventful for the hunters. I didn't go out again. I couldn't. The night before we were to leave it snowed. The woods looked beautiful, but I found out it's not good for the deer because they can be tracked more easily.

The hunters went out one more time that morning. As I sat in the cabin, I heard a shot. The guys came back to get the snowmobile to bring in the deer. Sue shot it. As they disappeared into the woods, all I could do was pray it wasn't 'my deer.' It wasn't long before I heard them coming back, so I put on my jacket and walked outside. The three of them were happy and proud as they dragged the hog-tied deer behind the snowmobile out of the woods, up to the cabin, and hung the carcass on the nail in the tree. I stayed long enough to make sure it wasn't my deer. It was about a year old, two little spikes sticking out of his head. Then I walked sadly back into the cabin.

I had seen my friends in another light that day. They weren't the same, or maybe it was me who wasn't the same. The picture of such an indignity to such a majestic animal stays with me still.

SERENDIPITY

One cold, crisp morning
Four figures quietly walking
Three hardened hunters
Ever on their guard
One neophyte, apprehensive

One cold, crisp morning
On the other side of the woods
Charlie, a magnificent buck, arising, wandering,
Apprehensively looking

One cold, crisp morning
Charlie and me not knowing how
our lives would intertwine
Destiny

One cold, crisp morning
Me in the oak tree
Looking, listening, waiting, contemplating
Charlie approaching
Snorting, looking up
Me looking down

One cold, crisp morning
Four eyes lock
Appreciative, momentous
Finding serenity
Finding my camera
The only shot taken that day

One cold, crisp morning
Stop, appreciate
Splendor

One cold, crisp morning
Years later
A cornfield up north
A Fawn running back and forth
Playing and snorting in the wind

A Doe looking on
Affectionately, cautiously
A Buck nowhere to be seen
But not far away,
Watching

One cold, crisp morning
Another chance
To stop, appreciate
Exquisiteness

PARTICIPANTS

Laura Hutten is a Reading Recovery teacher and Literacy Specialist in the Westwood Community School district. She is currently teaching at Daly Elementary School in Inkster. Laura's teaching history also includes six years of teaching second grade. She was instrumental in bringing the ideas of Lucy Calkins and Writer's Workshop to her district. Laura has been teaching for a total of fourteen years. She received her bachelor's degree in Education from Michigan State University, and returned there for her master's degree in Reading and Language Arts. Laura participated in MEAP Range finding in Lansing, which led her to the Meadow Brook Writing Project. She has been married to her husband Scott for six years, and they have a 20-month-old son, Lucas. Lucas is indeed the child of a reading teacher, as he already knows all of his letter sounds, and is speaking in complete sentences. Laura loves to run, and has completed the 26.2 mile Detroit Marathon. She also kick boxes, and watches the occasional soap opera.

Desiree Harrison is a graduate of University of Michigan with a degree in Elementary Education. She attended Michigan for five years and decided to be a teacher at the end of her junior year when she participated in an organization called Greening of Detroit, where she worked with kids at a camp, and realized that working with kids is what she was meant to do. Originally, she was going to be a pediatrician but decided she could work with kids in a different way, as a teacher. Desiree has been teaching seventh and eighth graders for two years now, and she is looking forward to teaching fifth graders in the fall of 2007. She still longs to be a journalist, however, so you may see her name in a column someday. Desiree heard about the Meadow Brook Writing Project through her friend and colleague Tre, and is very happy that she decided to be a part of the project. In the fall, she will not only be going back to school as a teacher, but also as a student as she begins earning her master's degree at Wayne State University in Instructional Technology. While she will be very busy, she still plans on finding time to go to the beach. Hopefully, she will find herself at Miami Beach again sometime soon.

Christina Fifield is a teacher for Farmington Public Schools. She is a seventh grade teacher and Literacy Coach at Warner Middle School. She also started their after school writing club. She has been at Warner for the last four years. The five years previously, she taught fourth and fifth grade at Wood Creek Elementary. She was also a student in both Warner and Wood Creek, and many of her current colleagues were once her teachers. Stepping into some classrooms, at times, gives her déjà vu. She graduated from Michigan State University. GO GREEN!!! At MSU she received her B.A. in English with her teaching certificate and her master's in Curriculum and Teaching. She has been married for almost a year to Scott, who is also a Farmington teacher. They are in the process of adopting their son from Guatemala. They are anxiously and excitedly awaiting his arrival and hoping he will be here by Christmas. Besides teaching, she enjoys reading and biking. She has even trekked across Europe on her bike. Christi is also passionate about animals and volunteered at an animal sanctuary in Utah.

Laura Amatulli is a dynamic teacher of sixth graders in her science and writing classes at the Avondale Meadows Upper Elementary School. Laura makes her classroom "the place to be" while in sixth grade. She teaches through the use of hands-on science experiments with follow-up writing assignments. Laura is the Student Council advisor and the leader of the Girls in Science Club at Avondale Meadows. She plans on using her Meadow Brook Writing Project experience and the connections she has made at OU to celebrate writing at Avondale Meadows by starting a writing circle with her students. Whether it is writing in science, for grants she has won, or while working with teachers at workshops she presents, Laura writes because she loves to. Her enthusiasm for writing is contagious, and the Meadow Brook Writing Project is richer because of her contributions. Laura stays busy outside of school also. She and her husband John are both proud of their ethnic heritage, so the Amatulli home is filled with Irish wit and Italian pride. Throw into the mix four children, Scott in high school, Ann Marie in sixth grade, Dominic in third grade, and two-year-old Lucas—Laura is one busy lady!

William (Bill) Byrne teaches rhetoric classes at Oakland University in Rochester, Michigan. He spent 17 years teaching high school in New York and New Jersey and then took a 30-year hiatus to work for Volkswagen of America in marketing and training. While working full time for VW, he kept his hand in teaching as an adjunct professor at several campuses of Oakland

Community College and Davenport University. He has published articles sporadically in *Training Magazine*, the *Journal for Technical Writing*, and *The Oakland Journal*, the professional publication for Oakland University. You can access his work through *The Oakland Journal's* archives. In the fall of 2007, his "Poems from the Workplace," which deal with some of his characterizations of his co-workers at Volkswagen, will be published in *The Oakland Journal*. His two sons are both talented professional musicians, and their work can be viewed at **http://www.andrewmbyrne.com/**and **http://www.davidgregorybyrne.com/**.

Kris McLaughlin has been teaching for ten years. She currently teaches third grade at Dodson Elementary in the Plymouth-Canton School District. Her mission is to create lifelong learners, just like herself. Kris' love of reading and writing has more than inspired her students. Her passion for writing has been usurped by her students, who sometime prefer missing recess to stay in her classroom to write! Kris has worked at a summer camp in Russia for the past six years. Her work there has spilled over to also working with orphanages. Kris went to Russia for the first time six years ago. She has gone several times but stayed in the U.S. to be part of the Meadow Brook Writing Project this year.

Elontra Hall is a gifted writer, talented violist, avid reader, and practically every student's favorite teacher. His multiple interests help him to write rich works full of masterfully threaded language and imagery. One of the concepts from the Meadow Brook writing project that he hopes to continue molding is the "River of Hidden Language." In this genre mix of prose and poetry, Elontra dabbles in the fundamental qualities of language's fluidity, divinity, birth, death, and never ending flow. Musical concepts have also been known to make their way into Elontra's works. And the lessons he's learned at Meadow Brook have found their way into his teaching style as well. Every term Elontra attempts to reach youth with the invaluable lessons learned through writers' workshop and how to express feelings through writing.

Katie Meister was raised in Detroit, Michigan. She was the fifth of seven siblings. She grew up traveling back and forth to her cottage in Canada that was about 33 miles from her house. Katie received her undergraduate degree in teaching from Central Michigan University. She later attained her master's degree in Reading at Oakland University. It was at Central Michigan that she met her husband of 27 years. He now works at GM as a design engineer. He is a published author and is currently working on a book. They have two sons, Justin and Phillip. Justin is a graduate from Michigan Tech and lives in

Wisconsin; while Philip is a graduate of the University of Michigan and is moving to Chicago. Katie worked in Houston Independent School District for 16 years. She taught everything from first grade through sixth by choice. This has given her a wealth of experiences that make her the dynamic teacher she is today. Michigan was blessed to have her move back in 1996. Her latest teaching position has been the last seven years in Hamtramck, which she enjoys very much. She has organized a chapter of the National Junior Honor Society at her school, Kosciuzko Middle School. She encourages the students to participate in a variety of leadership roles and plans many exciting activities as their advisor.

April Lewis will begin her tenth year of teaching this fall. Once again, she will be in the classroom teaching fifth graders at South Lyon Community Schools. The students are sure to love her as she has a great sense of humor and caring heart. She is a graduate of Michigan State University where she received her undergraduate degree in Elementary Education as well as a graduate degree in Curriculum and Teaching. These broad degrees have allowed her to teach several grades—first, second and fifth—of which fifth grade is her favorite. In her spare time she likes to snowmobile and travel to exciting places. In the near future she hopes to go to Ireland, Scotland, Australia and New Zealand. If April weren't in the classroom shaping young minds every day, she would consider a career as a CSI detective. She joined the Meadow Brook Writing Project after the encouragement of her friend and Writing Project colleague, Christi: "I'd heard about it before and thought that it would be fun. I love to write!"

John Callaghan is a veteran teacher. He teaches English at Dakota High School in Chippewa Valley Schools and has taught in the district since 1979. Before that he taught English and coached football and basketball at Gabriel Richard High School in Riverview, Michigan, from 1968 to 1979. His first teaching experience was at Brother Rice High School in Birmingham, Michigan, from 1962 to 1968. He taught English and Latin during those years and also coached the freshman football team. John is married to Mary Anne (Caroselli) since 1977. Mary Anne is a kindergarten teacher at Mohawk Elementary in Chippewa Valley Schools. John and Mary Anne have four children: John III, Joseph Silvio, Kevin Andrew, and Molly Elizabeth. John III and Joe are graduates of Chippewa Valley High School, and Kevin and Molly are graduates of Dakota High School. John III is almost finished with his physical education degree at Eastern Michigan University; Joe is a graduate of Eastern Michigan University (Telecommunications); Kevin is studying English at Western Michigan University and wants to teach high school English; and Molly is a senior at Michigan State University, majoring in psychology. John intends to keep on teaching, not only because he loves teaching but also because he has three children still in college.

Mary Cox is a teacher of 37 years who has been an active participant in the Writing Project for 20 years and is a director of the Meadow Brook Writing Project. She presently teaches at Renaissance High School. Her interests, besides her involvement in teaching, include reading, poetry, classical music, and walking on Belle Isle. She lives in Downtown Detroit with her two cats, Cleo and Stinky, overlooking the Detroit River.

Kathleen Reddy-Butkovich is a teacher in the Plymouth-Canton Community School District currently working as an ELA support teacher. The P-CCS District's focus on the English language arts offers many opportunities for professional study and classroom collaborations. Her work as associate director of the Meadow Brook Writing Project continues to inspire her learning, teaching, and writing.

Ronnelle G. Payne (Ronnie) has been teaching seventh and eighth grade Language Arts for ten years, but will embark on a new adventure this school year as a school administrator. Her students affectionately call her Major Payne. Her former school (Detroit Academy of Arts & Sciences) was a part of Edison Project where she was Curriculum Coordinator and a Nationally Certified Trainer with Edison Schools, Inc. Ronnie is also a professional speaker and conducts seminars and workshops on public speaking, effective listening skills, goal setting, and more. Ronnie never thought she'd end up teaching, but it was inevitable with a mom who has owned a business school for more than thirty years! Her mom, Freddie Payne, is co-owner of Payne-Pulliam School of Trade & Commerce in Detroit. She plans to join her mom in business adding after school tutoring, summer youth programs, and ACT preparation classes to its expansion. Ronnie keeps busy with her son Christian, being a Mary Kay consultant, and making jewelry. She even started a jewelry club with her students called G.E.M.S., Girls Empowered for Major Success.

Bonnie Cates is a Reading Recovery teacher and Reading Specialist at Highview Elementary in the Crestwood School District since 1975. She has two wonderful children: son, Dennis, currently serving in the U.S. Air Force; and daughter, Corinne, a graduate of Michigan State University, a high school history/French teacher, and now full time mother to Bonnie's two grandchildren, Will and Jessica. Twenty-one month old Will is the apple of

Bonnie's eye and four month Jessica is her little princess. While Bonnie enjoys spending as much time as she can, playing, reading, and singing with Will and Jessica, she still has time to quilt, crochet, read, and watch old movies. Family is very important to her, and she especially cherishes the too short times that her son comes home, and her whole family is together again.

Afterword

Under Siege

Callaghan was at it again. He and Mary were plotting something as usual. I decided to sit back and wait. It usually found its way to me anyway. Somehow or another they would need me for something, and I would get bullied into going along. Ronnie and Bonnie—yes, those are their real names—were chatting it up about one thing or another, and Bill was lecturing the Lauras on how to move around their targets without being heard. I had gotten the same instruction a couple of days before with Chris and Kristi.

The days were getting hotter, and our team hadn't heard anything from the Central Unit. We were all beginning to get a little anxious. April and our other superior officer, Kathleen, had been missing for a few days; and Katie kept us updated on any recon and information that was coming in regarding their whereabouts and recovery. I had told them that it was too early to try to test us in the field, that we needed more time in simulation, but who really listens to me anyway? I was glad that Desiree had stumbled into our unit. It gave me a sense of calm. We had been in the trenches together, fought side by side on the front lines, and I'm not embarrassed to say that she saved my bacon more than a few times. Eventually, Mary rounded all of us up and made us each give a status report on our various assignments.

"The details," Ronnie and Bonnie began, "that we have come across show us that we have a very small window of opportunity before we are discovered by the enemy and forced into a losing battle. "

Bill and the Lauras stressed the importance of making sure that we were able to blend in well with the surrounding area and people. "Otherwise, we can kiss our keisters goodbye," Bill finished.

139

April and Kathleen still hadn't been found, but there were reports of a woman that resembled April in a local "hospital," if it could be called that. Katie gave us intel on the place, and we concluded that it must be a detention center of some sort. She outlined an extraction plan, and we all agreed that we would help to refine it and liberate our comrade. Kris and Christi managed to get away with telling us only that the supplies were running low and that we would need to restock soon or begin to forage about the surrounding areas for comparable fare. We all knew that the second option wouldn't work well because the area had been torn to bits by the rebels and the allied forces. We were stuck in the middle of a war-zone. Desiree had deduced that by running operations at our current capacity, we were doomed to failure.

"So, Hall," Callaghan started, "what do you have to report?"

Through the gray hair matted on his forehead and hanging slightly in his line of vision, he stared at me. With eyes slit he scourged me. I could tell he hated my guts. Mary stood beside him, hopeful. Hopeful that this time she would be able to send me to the wolves outside. Beads of sweat began to run down my forehead. My nerves and the oppressive heat were starting to take a toll.

Finally, I resolved to open my mouth and tell them what I had, but just as I began to give my thoughts voice, Kathleen, guns drawn and smoking, burst into the compound.

"Incoming!" she yelled. We all hit the deck and listened with bated breath at the shelling that had begun anew. From that I could tell, it was going to be a long day...

by Elontra Hall

140